THE DARK KNIGHT LEGEND

THE DARK KNIGHT LEGEND
JUNIOR NOVEL

FROM THE FILMS
BATMAN BEGINS AND **THE DARK KNIGHT**
ADAPTED BY **STACIA DEUTSCH**

SCREENPLAYS BY
JONATHAN NOLAN, CHRISTOPHER NOLAN,
AND **DAVID S. GOYER**

STORIES BY
CHRISTOPHER NOLAN
AND **DAVID S. GOYER**

BATMAN CREATED BY **BOB KANE**

HARPER FESTIVAL
An Imprint of HarperCollinsPublishers

HarperFestival is an imprint of HarperCollins Publishers.

The Dark Knight Legend: Junior Novel

HARP26750
Library of Congress catalog card number: 2012934940
ISBN 978-0-06-213227-7
Book design by John Sazaklis
12 13 14 15 16   LP/BR   10 9 8 7 6 5 4 3 2 1
❖
First Edition

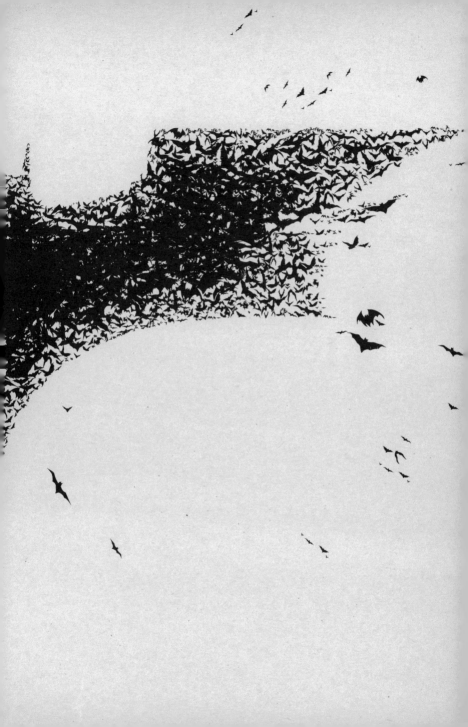

PROLOGUE

Bruce and his friend Rachel were playing hide-and-seek. Rachel knew her way around the large, rambling Wayne estate because her mother was its housekeeper. But Bruce still had places where Rachel wouldn't find him.

Beyond the greenhouse, there was an old stone well that hadn't been used in years. A few feet below the lip of the well was a platform of strong boards—just enough room for him to disappear.

Bruce didn't want to make a sound as he hopped into the well.

Crack!

Bruce shrieked as he plunged into the darkness and landed hard at the bottom of the pit.

His leg throbbed. Far above, he could hear Rachel screaming for him and he wished she'd hurry.

A frenzy of muffled screeching and movement filled Bruce with fear. The creatures that crowded the cavern had angry eyes and teeth like needles and they descended on him in an explosion of black. . . .

When Bruce awoke, it was night. Only Alfred, the family's butler, was in his room. "Took quite a fall, didn't we?" Alfred asked in his light cockney accent. "And why do we fall, Master Bruce?"

Bruce winced. He knew the answer but was unwilling to reply.

Alfred gave a patient smile, and answered the question himself. "So that we might better learn to pick ourselves up."

His leg aching, Bruce closed his eyes and nodded.

When his broken bone had healed, Bruce and his parents took the train into the city. The family stopped for a moment under the vaulted glass ceiling of Wayne Station. Everything in Gotham City—even the great Wayne Tower that rose above them in the center of it all—seemed to bear Bruce's last name. Bruce was proud of his family and what they had done for Gotham.

He did not love the opera his family was attending in honor of his mother's birthday, however. The music was interesting, and Bruce liked the witches gathered around the smoky cauldron. But the bats bursting from a hole on the stage were an unwelcome surprise.

Bruce knew they were fake, but it didn't matter. He felt light-headed. He could feel the claws. . . .

Grabbing his father's arm, Bruce begged, "Can we go?"

His father guided the family out of the theater through a side exit.

"Bruce, what's wrong?" his mother asked as they entered the alley.

"I just needed a bit of air, Martha," his father quickly cut in. "A bit of opera goes a long way. Right, Bruce?"

Bruce was grateful for his father's excuse. He wanted to be strong, but it was just so difficult. His father gave

Bruce a wink, and together they walked toward the main street.

A man suddenly appeared from the shadows. "Wallet! Jewelry!" He waved a gun.

Bruce froze; his knees locked.

"That's fine, just take it easy." The elder Wayne calmly handed Bruce his coat, then pulled out his wallet and handed it to the man.

The thief's hands were shaking, his eyes wild. "I said jewelry!" He reached forward for Bruce's mother's birthday gift, a beautiful strand of pearls.

Her husband stepped in front of her quickly. "Hey, just a—"

Bang!

Bruce flinched as his father slumped to the ground.

"Thomas!" Bruce's mother screamed, trying to hold her husband up. *"Thomas!"*

"Give me that necklace!" the man shouted.

Bang!

His mother lurched, and then fell. The thief grabbed at her necklace, but pearls clattered onto the pavement.

Bruce stared at the killer's face. He memorized every

wrinkle and hard edge. The man paused briefly, and then ran away to the street.

Bruce sank to his knees beside his parents.

The next few days were a blur. A detective named James Gordon promised to capture the killer. Richard Earle, Thomas Wayne's second-in-command at Wayne Enterprises, assured Bruce that the business would be waiting for him when he grew up. For an eight-year-old, that seemed very far away, and not at all real.

Bruce couldn't stop thinking about that night at the opera. "It was my fault," he told Alfred. "I made them leave the theater. If I hadn't gotten scared . . ."

Alfred comforted Bruce. "No," he said. "Nothing you did—nothing anyone ever did—can excuse that man. It's his fault, and his alone. Do you understand?"

Bruce sobbed. "I miss them, Alfred. I miss them so much!"

"So do I, Master Bruce," Alfred replied. "So do I."

ONE

After his parents' deaths, Bruce went away for school, and he didn't come back to Gotham until twelve years later. He had grown into a bitter, angry young man.

"You will be in the master bedroom, of course," Alfred said as Bruce settled in for the night at Wayne Manor. "It is, after all, your house."

Bruce did not like the idea of staying in his parents' room. "This isn't my house, Alfred. It's a mausoleum. A reminder of everything I lost. When I have my way, I'll pull the thing down brick by brick."

Alfred turned to face him. It was the first time Bruce had ever seen him angry. "This house, Master Wayne, has sheltered six generations of the Wayne family. It has stood by patiently while you've cavorted in and out of a dozen private schools and colleges. As have I. The Wayne family legacy is not so easily shrugged off."

Bruce replied softly, "I'm sorry to have disappointed you."

"Master Wayne," Alfred replied, "your father was a great man, but I have every confidence that you will exceed his greatness."

Bruce sighed. "Haven't given up on me yet?" he asked.

Alfred's answer was instant and unwavering. "Never."

At the sound of a car pulling into the driveway, Alfred went down to welcome Rachel Dawes.

Now assistant district attorney, Rachel was going to drive Bruce to the release hearing for his parents' killer, a small-time criminal named Joe Chill. Bruce had been planning for this day for years.

Bruce wrapped his jacket tightly around him and ran down to meet Rachel. "You look well," he said, stepping outside.

Pulling his gaze away from her face, Bruce asked, "Why is your boss letting Chill out of jail? My parents' killer . . ."

"In prison he shared a cell with Carmine Falcone, the mob boss," Rachel tried to explain. "He learned things, and he'll testify against Falcone in exchange for early parole."

A deal. Bruce could not believe that the man who had taken away his childhood was going to be set free because of some terrible deal.

He seethed with so much rage during the hearing, he had to leave the courtroom. Afterward, heading home, Bruce felt numb. "My parents deserved justice."

Rachel swerved off the highway, taking Bruce into a neighborhood he barely recognized. Years ago it had been a nice part of town. Now the streets were potholed, the buildings boarded up. Hollow-eyed senior citizens sat on the stoops, as shady young men worked deals on street corners.

"You care about justice?" Rachel asked him. "Look beyond your own pain, Bruce. This city is rotting. Chill is not the cause; he's the effect. Corruption is killing

Gotham. Falcone carries on flooding our city with crime and drugs—creating new Joe Chills. Falcone may not have killed your parents, Bruce, but he's destroying everything they stood for."

From there Rachel took Bruce straight to the Gotham Harbor docks. She parked near an unmarked door. Music blared from a basement club as a bouncer eyed them threateningly.

"They all know where to find Falcone," Rachel said. "But no one will touch him, because he keeps the bad people rich and the good people scared. What chance does Gotham have when the good people do nothing?"

Bruce got out of the car, and Rachel drove away, leaving him on the sidewalk.

Bruce went into the nightclub and waited to confront Gotham's mob boss.

"The little rich kid," Falcone said, eyeing Bruce with amusement. The bouncer knocked Bruce to the ground. Falcone stood over him. "You don't belong down here, kid. We don't play fair. You miss your mommy and daddy? Come down here again—I'll send you to them."

Falcone's goon threw Bruce outside. He struggled to his feet and staggered along the docks.

Bruce looked around. Workers were loading cargo onto a freighter about to depart. Quickly taking a wad of money from his wallet, Bruce handed it all to a homeless man. "Sell me your jacket."

The shocked man removed his raggedy coat. Then Bruce handed the man the dress coat he had been wearing, with all his money. He then dropped his empty wallet—and his tie—into the homeless man's fire.

He no longer wanted to be Bruce Wayne. He needed to become someone else. There were things Bruce needed to learn.

He slipped into the tattered jacket and headed toward the freighter. . . .

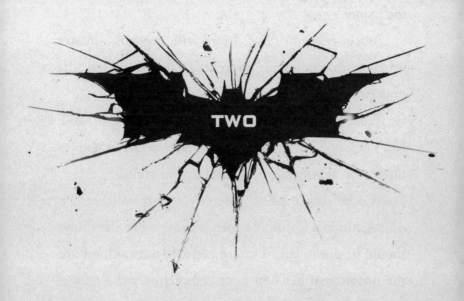

TWO

Bruce traveled the world for years searching for answers. It somehow seemed right that he ended up in a miserable prison half a world away from Gotham City.

The guard led Bruce to his cell and threw him onto the floor before slamming the door shut.

"These men have mistaken you for a criminal, Mr. Wayne," a voice said in the darkness. Bruce spun around to see who was speaking.

The man was well dressed. "My name is Henri

Ducard, but I speak for Rā's al Ghūl. Have you heard the name?"

Bruce replied, "I've heard the legends—master warrior, international mercenary, feared by all the underworld. Some even swear he's immortal."

"You have not escaped his notice," Ducard said. "Rā's al Ghūl and his League of Shadows offer a path to those who are capable of upholding our code."

"Code?" Bruce asked. "Aren't you criminals?"

"A criminal is simply a man who someone else thinks should be put in jail." Ducard gestured outward, toward the prison guards. "Our code respects only the natural order of things. We're not bound by their hypocrisy. Are you?"

Without waiting for an answer, Ducard walked to the cell door and knocked sharply. Instantly a guard pulled it open. "Tomorrow you will be released," Ducard said, pausing in the doorway. "A blue, double-bloomed poppy grows on the eastern slope of this mountain. If you can carry the flower to the top, you may find what you are looking for."

"And what am I looking for?" Bruce asked.

Ducard replied, "Purpose."

On the slope, exactly where Ducard had said, a field of blue poppies stretched to the horizon. Bruce picked one, looked up toward the mountain's icy peak and began walking. With each mile Bruce felt farther from—not closer to—the top.

When he finally entered the monastery at the peak, Bruce found a robed figure seated atop a platform. "Rā's al Ghūl?" Bruce rasped.

Ninja warriors stepped from the shadows, bows and swords primed. Shaking, Bruce held out the poppy.

Rā's al Ghūl began to speak in his native language, as Ducard stepped into the light and translated: "We will help you conquer your fear. In exchange you will renounce the cities of man. You will live in solitude. You will be a member of the League of Shadows." Ducard took the flower and inserted it into Bruce's lapel. "Are you ready to begin?"

Before Bruce could answer, Ducard kicked him to the floor. Bruce fought back, but he was no match for his opponent. He had a fighter's determination, but not the skill.

Days later, Ducard led his student to the edge of a frozen lake, where he handed Bruce a sword and a long silver glove with sharp hooks—a protective gauntlet.

They circled each other, the wind blowing harshly in Bruce's ear.

Ducard struck first, but Bruce parried with his gauntlet, leaping away.

Below him the ice cracked.

"Mind your surroundings," Ducard warned. "Always."

Bruce lunged—but Ducard blocked with *his* gauntlet, catching Bruce's thrust in his hooks. "Your parents' deaths were not your fault," he said, wrenching the sword from Bruce's grip and flinging it away. "They were your father's. He failed to act."

This comment enraged Bruce. He leaped at Ducard's throat—but Ducard ducked away, grabbing Bruce by his tunic. "The man had a gun!" Bruce growled.

"The will to take control is everything," Ducard said. "Your father trusted his city, its logic. He thought he understood the attacker and could simply give him what he wanted."

No, thought Bruce. *It wasn't my father's fault.* He

pushed away from Ducard.

"Your father did not understand the forces of decay," Ducard continued. "Cities like Gotham are in their death throes—chaotic, grotesque, beyond saving."

"Beyond saving?" Bruce asked. "You believe that?"

Ducard gazed out over the stark whiteness of the landscape. "It is not right that one must come so far to see the world as it is meant to be—pure, serene, solitary. These are the qualities we hold dear. But the important thing is whether *you* believe it. Can Gotham be saved, or is she an ailing ancestor whose time has run out?" With a sudden motion, Ducard struck with his sword.

Bruce grabbed the sword and swung a low, swift blow at Ducard's feet.

Ducard jumped, but not quickly enough, slipping to the ice. Bruce stood over him, touching the tip of his sword to Ducard's throat. "Yield," he said.

"You haven't beaten me. You've sacrificed sure footing for a killing stroke." Calmly Ducard tapped his sword near Bruce's feet.

Crack!

Bruce fell through the surface, into the black water beneath.

Having endured years of training, Bruce was finally to be inducted into the League of Shadows. The ceremony was to take place in the monastery's throne room. He wore a black ninja uniform, as did his teacher.

In a mortar on the altar, Ducard ground the dried poppy flower that Bruce had picked on his trek up the mountain. He poured the dust carefully into a small burner and lit it. "Drink in your fears," Ducard said as the smoke rose in silvery wisps. "Face them."

Bruce inhaled the foul smoke. He began to have flashbacks—the bats, his parents' deaths, Chill, Falcone. Bruce was afraid.

"To conquer fear, you must *become* fear," said Ducard. "You must bask in the fear of other men . . . and men fear most what they cannot see."

Ducard put on a mask and motioned for Bruce to do the same. Around them men stepped out of the darkness—dozens of them, identically masked and cloaked. "It is not enough to be a man," Ducard called out. "You must become an idea. A terrible thought. A *wraith*."

Ducard swung his sword at Bruce's head. With quick

reflexes Bruce leaped safely away.

"Face your fear . . ." Ducard's voice was distant, ghostly. Bruce approached a nearby chest and carefully lifted the lid.

Whoosh.

Hundreds of bats burst upward, shrieking, clawing at Bruce's face. He hid himself among the ninjas.

In the shadow of the bats, Ducard attacked again. "Become one with the darkness, Bruce Wayne," he said, placing his sword against a cloaked throat. "You cannot leave any sign."

A voice behind him replied, "I haven't."

Ducard whirled around in surprise. The ninja at the tip of his blade was not Bruce Wayne. Bruce had fooled him. Ducard was pleased.

In the center of the room, near a burning candle, Rā's al Ghūl appeared. "We have purged your fear. You are ready to lead these men. You are ready to become a member of the League of Shadows."

"By blowing out this candle," Ducard continued, "you renounce your mortal life. You renounce forever the cities of man. You dedicate your life to solitude."

Bruce leaned forward obediently, and then eyed the

sea of silent disciples. "Where will I be leading these men?"

"To Gotham," Ducard replied. "You yourself are a victim of Gotham's decay. That is why you came here, and that is why you must go back. You will assume the mantle of your birthright. As Gotham's favored son, you will be ideally placed."

"For what?" Bruce asked.

"To help us destroy the city," Ducard explained. "When Gotham falls, the other cities will follow."

Bruce couldn't believe what he heard. These men expected him to destroy what his family had built?

Bruce unsheathed his sword. Leaping to his feet, he tipped the candle to the floor. Fire ignited the wood planks and began to spread.

"What are you doing!" Ducard exclaimed.

"What's necessary." Bruce struck Ducard in the head with the butt of his weapon.

Fire exploded around them, broken wood and glass flying like shrapnel. Ninjas jumped to the floor, engulfed in fire. With a loud crack, a section of the roof tumbled toward them.

Bruce leaped away, but Rā's al Ghūl was crushed.

Bruce carried his unconscious trainer out the front door and onto the frozen slope. He left Ducard with an old man in a hut.

And then Bruce Wayne went home.

THREE

B ruce looked out the window of the private jet as it circled Gotham City. He felt, as always, grateful to Alfred. He'd received Bruce's phone call and had instantly flown to Asia to collect him.

"Alfred," Bruce said, "Gotham needs a symbol."

"What . . . *symbol*, sir?"

"Something for the good to rally behind," Bruce replied, "and the criminals to fear. . . ."

The next morning, Mr. Earle was presiding over a board meeting at Wayne Enterprises.

"Sorry to barge in," Bruce suddenly interrupted, "but I was in the area."

Earle's face went pale. "My boy!" he exclaimed, forcing a smile and rushing to shake Bruce's hand. "We thought you were gone for good!"

"Actually, I've come to work," Bruce replied. "I thought I'd find out what we actually *do* around here."

Bruce was soon given a tour of the business. The Applied Sciences department was the last stop, and Bruce went there alone, knowing that he needed time to speak to the department manager, Lucius Fox.

Fox showed Bruce all sorts of inventions, like a bulletproof bodysuit made of silicone over jointed armor. "I want to borrow it," Bruce said, feeling the suit's fibers. "For spelunking. Cave diving."

Fox raised an eyebrow. "You get a lot of gunfire down in those caves?"

There was a cavern below the southeast corner of Wayne Manor. It was unused and decaying; the only things living there were the bats. A small abandoned elevator, once used to carry goods up into the main living quarters, was boarded up.

The space was perfect. With a little renovation, Bruce would make it his lair.

He had a suit, a cave, Alfred to assist him. . . . Next, Bruce needed to find one honest cop.

Using darkness as his cover and wearing the black bodysuit, Bruce slipped into the office of Sergeant James Gordon, the man who so many years ago had shown him kindness after his parents' murder.

Disguising his voice and keeping his face hidden, Bruce said, "You're a good cop. One of the few. What would it take to get Carmine Falcone? He brings in shipments of drugs every week, yet nobody takes him down. Why?"

Gordon shrugged. "He's paid up with the right people. To get him, it would take leverage on Judge Faden. And a DA brave enough to prosecute."

"That would be Rachel Dawes, Finch's assistant DA. Watch for a sign."

"Who are you?" Gordon demanded. "Are you just one man?"

"Now we are two," Bruce said, and without a sound he disappeared.

The next day, Bruce returned to Applied Sciences. He needed more gear.

Fox gave him a wry look. "What is it today, more spelunking?"

Bruce said, "I need a lightweight grapnel hook. For climbing."

"We've got suction pads, grapnels . . . and this thing's pretty neat." From a box Fox pulled out a bronze contraption with a shoulder harness and belt. It looked like a parachute harness.

Fox headed for the door. "Come on, I'll show you something."

They walked out to a loading dock, where Fox lifted a sheet of black fabric from a crate. "Memory fabric." He took a glove from the same crate and slipped it onto his hand. Small electrodes protruded from the glove's fingers. "Flexible ordinarily, but if you put a current through it, the molecules align and become rigid."

Fox grabbed the fabric and it instantly popped into the shape of a small tent. "It could be tailored to any structure based on a rigid skeleton," he said.

Bruce felt its strength. It was impressive. But Bruce

was distracted by the sight of a vehicle with enormous tires, covered by a tarp. "What's that?" he asked.

"The Tumbler? Oh, you wouldn't be interested in *that* . . ."

Moments later, Bruce was taking Fox for a high-speed spin along a test track. The Tumbler was a cross between a sports car and a tank, and it drove like a dream. To the right of the usual driving position was a cockpit enclosed in a glass bubble with separate controls and video panels.

Fox pointed to a button on the center panel. "You hit that and it will boost her into a rampless jump."

After a few more turns, Bruce brought the Tumbler to a squealing, sudden halt.

"Well," Fox said, looking a little queasy, "what do you think?"

"Does it come in black?" Bruce asked with a smile.

FOUR

B ruce was a creature of the night now, a new person with a new name—Batman.

Batman was going to take Falcone and the mob down. He was going to reclaim Gotham City and make it safe once more.

Bruce had done his research. Falcone supplied drugs to the city, while a corrupt cop named Flass helped him escape the law. Judge Faden was also involved, keeping control over the city's criminal laws.

Bruce was certain that there was someone else, someone

working behind the scenes. Once Bruce found that person, he'd be closer to the source of the real problems.

That night, hidden from view, hanging upside down, Batman watched workers unload containers at a warehouse on a Gotham dock. When he shifted position, one of the workers looked up. The man didn't have enough time to scream before Batman attacked. Unaware that his workers were being taken out one by one, Carmine Falcone was in his office inside, having a meeting with Dr. Jonathan Crane, a thin man with glasses.

"You know who we're working for," Dr. Crane said without using the name of the mysterious man behind the drug smuggling. "When *he* gets here, *he* won't want to hear that you've been endangering our operation just to filch a few dollars from your dealers."

Falcone's thick face twitched. "He's coming to Gotham?"

"Soon," Crane replied. "This is our last shipment."

A distant yell shattered the night's silence. Falcone reached for his shotgun, and Flass bolted out the door to investigate.

Rat-ta-ta-ta-ta-ta-tat!

Hearing the sudden blast, Flass ducked behind a stack of shipping containers. Falcone ran up beside him.

Crane slipped out the office door and disappeared into the night.

After another scream, Flass jumped into his patrol car and drove away.

Falcone crept along the container stacks. The shipment had to be protected at all costs. He rounded a corner to find five of his men in a circle looking out, weapons in hand and tensed.

From the steel beams overhead, a shadow dropped into their midst: a man dressed like a giant bat. In seconds, with no weapon at all, he took out all five mob thugs.

As the caped figure stood over the men, Falcone asked, "What *are* you?"

The man turned slowly. "I'm Batman," he said.

A short time later, Sergeant Gordon stared in awe at the scene—Falcone's thugs knocked out, tied up, and sitting against a shipping container full of drugs. A line of cops held back the press photographers.

"Falcone's men?" asked a beat cop.

Gordon shrugged. "Does it matter? We'll never tie him to it anyway."

"I wouldn't be too sure of that," the cop replied, pointing upward.

Gordon followed his gesture to a huge harbor light beaming over the river. Strapped to the searchlight's enormous lens was Carmine Falcone—arms stretched outward. His sleeves had been ripped in a jagged pattern.

The light's beam shone on a cloud. It made a circle of light, surrounding the silhouette of a bat—the city's new symbol.

FIVE

Dr. Crane was the director of the Arkham Asylum. The fortress—located on an island called the Narrows—held some of the most mentally unstable criminals in Gotham history.

Crane was called into the county jail to evaluate whether or not Falcone was insane. No one knew that just the night before, the doctor had been in the mob boss's office on personal business.

"I know about your experiments on the inmates at your nuthouse," Carmine Falcone threatened. He wanted Crane to get him out of jail. "So what's hidden in the drugs I bring for you?"

"If *he* wanted you to know, he'd have told you himself."

"I've been smuggling your stuff for months. He's got something big planned. I want in."

Crane didn't respond to Falcone's threats. Instead he pulled out a burlap sack with eyeholes, stitching for a mouth, and a plastic breathing tube. He put it on. "I use this in my experiments. Those crazies, they can't stand it. . . ."

Whoosh.

White smoke shot out of Crane's briefcase.

Falcone started to hallucinate. The crime boss saw lizard tongues, sharp and forked, flicking out of Crane's mask holes.

Falcone let out a piercing scream.

The prison official ran to the door. "Oh, he's not faking," Crane said gravely, stepping into the hallway. Falcone wasn't crazy before. But he was now. "I'll talk to the judge."

Bruce Wayne felt that to keep his new identity a secret, he had to go around town acting like a rich, spoiled playboy. He wanted everyone to think that there was no way he and Batman could possibly be the same man. So he invited two beautiful women to have a lavish dinner with him at the Gotham Plaza Hotel.

As the group was leaving, Bruce was certain that his bad-boy reputation was secure. At the entrance he ran into his old friend Rachel Dawes. He hadn't seen her in more than eight years, and he was embarrassed by the way he was acting.

"I . . . I'd heard you were back," Rachel said, eyeing the two women. "Where were you?"

"Oh, kind of all over," Bruce replied nervously. "You know."

"No, Bruce, I don't know," Rachel replied. "Neither did a lot of people. People who thought you were probably dead. Me, I never quite gave up on you."

"Come on, Bruce!" one of the women said, snuggling into his shoulder. "Let's party!"

Bruce cringed. "Rachel . . . that's not me. Inside I'm different. I'm—"

"The same great little kid you used to be?" She poked him softly on the chest. "Bruce, it's not who you are underneath, but what you *do* that defines you."

She walked away.

Rain fell while Batman hunched on a fourth-story ledge between buildings on a near-deserted Gotham street.

As Detective Flass approached, Batman fired his grapnel gun. The wire wrapped around the cop's ankle, lifting him off the ground.

"Who was with Falcone at the docks?" Batman demanded, drawing the detective upward so they were eye to eye.

"I never knew his name!" Flass screamed. "There was something hidden in the drugs. . . ."

"What?"

"I don't know—*something*! I never went to the drop-off; it's in the Narrows."

Batman leaned in closer, and let Flass safely drop to the ground.

Following Flass's tip, Batman discovered a large shipping crate behind Arkham Asylum. Inside was an industrial machine the size of a small van. A label on its side read WAYNE ENTERPRISES: M-EMIT.42B. He didn't know what he'd discovered, but he knew it was important.

He ducked into the shadows as he heard footsteps.

Two dockworkers appeared, along with a thin man wearing glasses.

"The boss wants you to keep it in the asylum until the time comes, Dr. Crane," the first worker said.

Batman snuck in closer. Too close. It was a mistake. Dr. Crane saw him. There was no way to escape before Crane released the same gas he'd used to poison Falcone.

The nightmares began immediately: Rā's al Ghūl . . . the wooden chest . . . bats . . . the monastery in flames . . .

Flames. His memory and reality were blurred as Crane set the ground on fire.

Rolling along the rain-soaked sidewalk, Batman managed to put out the blaze. Then, summoning what was left of his will, he shot the grapnel gun upward and lifted himself onto a roof, out of sight.

Reaching into his Utility Belt for his phone, Batman punched in a number and grunted, "Alfred . . . come . . . poisoned . . . need a blood sample . . ."

When Bruce woke up two days later, it was his birthday.

"I only breathed the slightest amount of gas," Bruce

explained to Alfred. The experience had felt familiar. . . .

"I took a blood sample and sent it to a laboratory known for both discreet and prompt blood work," Alfred said, taking a sheet of paper from the night table.

Bruce read the report. "'Protein-based compounds . . . It might be possible to make an antidote. I think I know how to do it."

SIX

The next day, Bruce showed the report to Fox. The man's eyes widened in disbelief. "*This* was in your blood?"

"It's some kind of weaponized hallucinogen," Bruce replied. "Administered in aerosol form. Could you synthesize an antidote?"

"This receptor's a compound I've never seen before," Fox replied. "I can do it—but it'll be hard."

Bruce nodded gratefully. "One more thing. Do you know what a Wayne Enterprises M-Emit forty-two B is?"

Fox sat at his desk and typed the name into his computer. "Hmm . . . it won't tell us. Must be a defense prototype. I'll make a couple calls."

Bruce's birthday party was starting without him. Batman was perched on a landing outside Dr. Crane's office at Arkham Asylum.

Rachel was inside with Crane. Through the transmitter embedded in his cowl, Batman could hear their two voices clearly.

"Dr. Crane," Rachel said, "about the Falcone report you filed with the judge: Isn't it unusual for a fifty-eight-year-old man with no history of mental illness to have a complete psychotic break?" She was there to investigate the reason Falcone had been moved from the jail to the asylum.

"Look, I doubt we're even supposed to be having this conversation," Crane said gravely. "But off the record, we're not talking about easily manufactured eccentricities. Come, I'll show you."

Using his spikes, his instincts, and occasional peeks into asylum windows, Batman trailed the pair to a dismal cell. Inside, Carmine Falcone lay strapped to a bed, mumbling, "Scarecrow . . . s-scarecrow . . . s-s . . ."

A few moments later Rachel and Crane walked off the elevator into an old, musty hallway.

"This is where we make our medicine," Dr. Crane said. "Perhaps you can have some. Clear your head."

As a puff of gas blew into her face, Rachel screamed and fell to the floor.

Thunk.

The overhead lights went out, plunging the room into darkness.

A window shattered.

Batman attacked two workers—one with a grapnel hook around the ankles and the other with a knockout punch.

Batman spun around to fight Crane. He was wearing the Scarecrow gas mask.

A puff of poison came from the mask, but Batman ducked in time. Tearing open Crane's jacket, Batman lifted up a container full of toxin attached to a tube that ran up the jacket's sleeve. "Taste of your own medicine, Doctor?" he asked.

Crane's eyes bugged out in terror as Batman squeezed the container.

Tsssss . . .

Crane fell to the ground, gagging.

"Who are you working for?" Batman demanded.

"R-R-Rā's," Crane stammered. "Rā's . . . al Ghūl!"

Batman pulled Crane tight. "Rā's al Ghūl is dead, Crane! Who are you *really* working for?"

Crane's eyes suddenly glazed over. "Dr. Crane isn't here right now," he babbled, "but if you'd like to make an appointment—"

Crane had lost it. He was useless. Batman dropped him and turned around. He scooped up Rachel and rose. Through the window he could see dozens of police cars. He had to get out before he was arrested.

Not knowing his motives, the Gotham police department considered Batman to be a dangerous vigilante, and they were looking for him.

Using his cloak and grapnel hook, Batman escaped to the Batmobile. He secured Rachel in the passenger seat.

A helicopter tracked them from overhead. A car cut them off in front. Batman nailed the accelerator.

Whump!

His tires rolled up and over the car, crushing it. Batman fired his rockets, and they landed with a thud on the roof of a parking garage. With another thrust of the rockets, they launched onto the highway, thumping down into the center lane. Batman lunged into the pod seat. Swerving down the next exit ramp, the Batmobile screeched onto the road and plunged into a wooded area.

"Hold on!" he told Rachel. She twisted in her seat, cowering.

The Batmobile shot forward, its wheels spinning, arcing high through the air, over the river—and plunging straight into the face of a waterfall!

The water's powerful crash drowned out Rachel's scream. The Batmobile thumped onto a solid floor inside the Batcave. Batman hooked a steel cable, and ground anchors yanked the car to a halt.

He lifted Rachel from the cockpit and carried her into the cavern. Hoping it wasn't too late, Batman reached for the antidote.

Rachel's head pounded. Forcing her eyes open, she looked into the mask of Batman.

"Where are we?" she asked. "Why did you bring me here?"

"If I hadn't, your mind would be lost," Batman replied. "You were poisoned."

"I remember . . . nightmares. The mask . . . it was Crane! I have to tell the police—" She stumbled, trying to get up.

Batman caught her. "Rest first."

She tried to look into his face, to see his eyes, but he was backing away. . . . "Why did you save my life?" Rachel asked, watching his silhouette.

"Gotham needs you," he replied.

"And you serve Gotham?"

"I serve justice."

"Perhaps you do," she said softly.

"I'm going to give you a sedative to put you back to sleep," Batman said, holding up the two vials. "You'll wake up back at home, and when you do, go to the asylum. Get these to Gordon. Trust no one else."

"What are they?" Rachel asked.

"The antidote. One for Gordon to inoculate himself. I'm certain he will need it. The other should be used to start mass production. Crane was just a pawn," he said. "He was working for someone else."

As Batman stepped closer with her sedative, Rachel closed her eyes. She trusted him, and she could use the sleep.

SEVEN

After changing into a white shirt and dinner jacket, Bruce took the elevator up from the Batcave and emerged into his study through a secret revolving bookcase. His birthday party was in full swing. He would show up for a bit and then leave. He had a long night ahead of him.

"Rachel's sedated," Bruce told Alfred. "You can take her home. Is Fox still here?"

Alfred nodded toward the crowd, where Fox hovered at the buffet. Bruce was headed toward him when suddenly a guest shouted, "There he is!" Voices began singing "Happy Birthday."

Shaking hands and grinning, Bruce moved through the crowd. When he finally reached Fox, Bruce whispered, "Any word on that . . . item?"

Fox replied, "My contact in heavy weapons says it's a microwave emitter. It vaporizes water."

Bruce's mind raced. Vaporizing water was harmless—but other substances, when changed from liquid to gas, could be lethal.

"Could you use the emitter to put a biological agent into the air?" Bruce asked.

"Sure, if the water supply were poisoned before you vaporized it," Fox said.

If the drug that Crane was using had been dumped into the water supply, no one would be affected by drinking it. But if the water became vapor, then the entire city could be poisoned. . . .

As Bruce realized the horror of what could happen, Mr. Earle called out behind him.

"Happy birthday, Bruce—not everybody thought you'd make it this far!"

"Sorry to disappoint," Bruce said, turning around.

He was anxious to get away, but he didn't want to scare his guests. He needed to talk with Fox for a while longer.

Bruce finally excused himself when a woman grabbed his arm. Mrs. Delane was an old friend of the family. "Bruce!" her fluty voice piped. "There's somebody here you simply *must* meet!"

"I can't just now—" Bruce protested, but he immediately swallowed his words. With her was a man wearing a blue poppy on his jacket.

"Now, am I pronouncing it right?" Mrs. Delane trilled. "Mr. Rā's al Ghūl?"

Bruce faced the man only to realize that Henri Ducard was not who he had claimed to be. Ducard, in fact, had been Rā's al Ghūl all along.

"Surely you don't begrudge me dual identities?" Rā's al Ghūl asked. "You were my greatest student . . . until you betrayed me."

Bruce suddenly became aware of people who didn't belong at the party—members of the League of Shadows, dressed as waiters and busboys.

The guests were in danger. Bruce had to protect them. Thinking fast, he clinked a glass and began to insult his guests, calling them leeches—people who wanted to use their connection to the Wayne name for their own glory. In minutes, angry people were in their cars, driving away. It didn't take long to clear the house.

"They don't have long to live," Rā's al Ghūl said with amusement. "Your antics at the asylum have forced my hand."

Bruce began piecing together the puzzle. "Crane was working for *you*!"

Rā's al Ghūl nodded. "His toxin is derived from our blue poppies."

"You're going to unleash Crane's poison on the entire city—and destroy millions of lives!"

"No. Billions of lives. Gotham will tear itself apart through fear—but that will just be the beginning. The world will watch in terror as the greatest city falls. Anarchy and chaos will spread. Mankind will ravage itself, the species will be culled . . . and the balance of nature will be restored. The planet will be saved."

Bruce couldn't believe what he was hearing. "You're inhuman!"

"Don't question my humanity, Bruce," Rā's al Ghūl said. "I saved you. I showed you a path and took away your fear. *I made you what you are.* And in return you attacked me and burned my home. Since then you've used my skills and techniques to interfere with my plans, plans in which you were supposed to play a part."

He nodded to his men. They began setting fire to the drapes.

"You were supposed to be Gotham's destroyer. Instead you became her only protector," Rā's al Ghūl said.

"You underestimate Gotham!"

"Gotham is helpless without you. That's why I'm here. We've infiltrated every aspect of the city's infrastructure. *You* underestimate Gotham's corruption," Rā's al Ghūl said. He knocked Bruce unconscious.

EIGHT

Miles away, at Arkham Asylum, four armed SWAT team members stood guarding Wayne Enterprises' stolen microwave emitter. One of them checked his watch and nodded to a partner, who quickly powered up the machine. Moving with ninja precision, the men began placing explosive charges along the wall.

At the same time, high above the street level, Rā's al Ghūl's people took over the train system. The city ground to a halt.

Meanwhile, Alfred found Bruce pinned under a burning ceiling beam.

"*Master Wayne!*" Alfred slapped the young man's face until his eyes finally flickered.

With a grunt, Bruce pushed upward. The beam jerked—and then crashed beside him onto the floor.

Bruce pressed four keys on the piano—the combination that made the bookcase swing open. The two men ducked inside the elevator, then dropped downward into the coolness of the Batcave.

As they landed, Bruce winced at the sound of crashing timbers above. "What have I done, Alfred?" he whispered. "Everything my father and his father built . . ."

Alfred took a deep, sorrowful breath. "The Wayne legacy," he said, "is more than bricks and mortar, sir."

"I thought I could help Gotham," Bruce said. "But I've failed."

Alfred looked hard into the young man's face and said, "Why do we fall, sir?"

Bruce knew the answer: "So that we might better learn to pick ourselves up." He then asked Alfred, "Still haven't given up on me?"

"Never."

Alfred helped Batman prepare for duty.

Back at Arkham, someone had set the inmates free and they were rioting. At the same time, Rachel was trying to find Sergeant Gordon to give him the antidote that Batman had supplied her.

Dr. Crane approached her on a police horse. He was cackling, the burlap mask firmly on his face. "Crane!" she cried out.

He hissed, *"Scarecrow!"*

At the sound of gunshots, the horse startled. It threw the Scarecrow off its back and took off in a gallop, dragging Crane on the ground by his stirrups.

Rachel raced around the building and found Gordon, coughing and choking. He turned to her, his eyes wide with fright.

She knew from his expression that he'd inhaled some of the poison. "Gordon, it's me, Rachel! I have the antidote! Stay calm," she said. "I can help you." She gave him the cure.

Gordon's eyes flashed. "Rachel?"

Inmates rushed them.

Woom!

The Batmobile hurtled from out of the cloud. It skidded to a stop inches from Rachel.

The inmates dived away as the door flew open and Batman jumped out. A brick clipped him on the side of his mask. Shrieking and frightened, the inmates went after Batman, throwing whatever they could find.

Certain that Gordon could handle himself, Batman distracted the inmates as he lifted Rachel off the ground. He fired his grapnel gun upward, and they soared into the air onto one of the towering spires of Arkham Asylum.

From the rooftop Rachel could see all of Gotham.

"They're going to unleash the toxin on the entire city," Batman said. "I have to find the microwave emitter."

"They're lifting a machine up to the tracks!" Rachel blurted. She pointed to the elevated train.

A metallic noise screeched as the train began to inch forward.

Batman tensed, his eyes following the track's path into the heart of Gotham. "Of course! The track runs directly over the water mains! If he crashes that thing into Wayne Tower, it'll blow the central hub, and create enough toxin to blanket the entire city!"

Batman stepped to the roof's edge. The train was several stories below, pulling farther away.

"Wait!" Rachel cried. As he turned, she reached up to his face. "You could die. At least tell me your name."

"It's not who I am underneath," he said, "but what I *do* that defines me."

Her words.

"Bruce," she said. But he was gone, falling into the mist.

NINE

Batman held out his arms. Controlling his cape, he caught the wind and sailed into the clear air over the Gotham River. The tracks were below him. He angled toward them, gliding until he was over the train's engine.

Inside, Rā's al Ghūl turned in surprise. "You!" he exclaimed.

Batman dropped onto the roof, and Rā's al Ghūl scrambled outside.

Batman lunged. With a sword in one hand and a

cane in the other, Rā's al Ghūl held him off, swinging wildly.

As they sped through a tunnel, Batman caught the cane in the hooks of his gauntlet. He lifted his arm upward, and the cane went flying.

"Familiar," Rā's al Ghūl said mockingly. He thrust the sword, and Batman jumped. Batman's foot slipped on the slick surface, and he lost balance.

Rā's al Ghūl took advantage. He raised the sword over his nemesis's head—

Chank.

Batman crossed both his arms in front, and the sword stuck fast in the hooks of both his gauntlets.

"Don't you have anything new?" Rā's al Ghūl taunted.

"How about *this*?" Batman said, yanking his arms in opposite directions.

Rā's al Ghūl's sword split in two, and he stumbled back from the force of the jolt.

Batman spun around. Wayne Tower was close. He dropped to his stomach, leaning over the front of the train. Aiming carefully, he shot his grapnel gun cable into the car's guide wheels.

Its wheels sparking and screeching, the train slowed but didn't stop. It wasn't going to be enough. The cable wouldn't hold.

"What are you doing?" Rā's al Ghūl shouted from behind him.

"What's necessary," Batman replied.

He threw the entire grapnel gun apparatus into the path of the guide wheel. The train lurched, hopping off its rail, smashing against the concrete guides.

Rā's al Ghūl dived onto Batman, pinning him against the roof. Batman rolled upright, but Rā's al Ghūl's grip was tight.

"Are you afraid?" Rā's al Ghūl hissed.

"Yes," Batman rasped, his strength ebbing. He loosened his own grip and slipped his hand down his cloak to the activating pockets. "But not of you."

The cloak went rigid. It caught the wind of the still-moving train, and Batman was yanked upward, into the air.

Rā's al Ghūl looked up in surprise, anger, and terror.

With a horrible noise, the train broke through the guide rail. It plunged to the street, speeding toward Wayne Tower.

Crash!

The impact shook the ground as the train exploded into flames, taking Rā's al Ghūl with it.

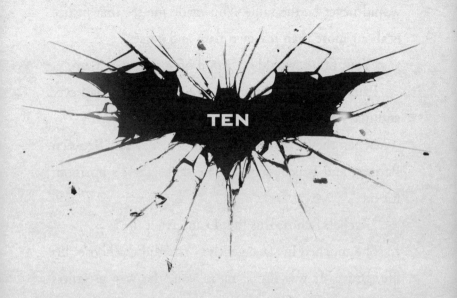

TEN

A few days later, with the mob weakened and Falcone off the streets, Gotham seemed like a place worth saving, and people were rolling up their sleeves to help.

Bruce's home was a smoking skeleton of twisted steel among piles of stone. Inside, Alfred supervised salvage workers.

Bruce heard footsteps and glanced up to see Rachel approaching. He was happy to see her. "Do you remember the day I fell?" he asked.

"Of course," Rachel replied.

"As I lay there, I *knew* . . . I could sense that things would never be the same. You made me see that justice is about more than my own pain and anger."

"Your father would be proud of you. Just as I am."

Bruce stopped. Feeling as if everything he had ever endured had been for this moment, he kissed her.

When they separated, Rachel turned away. "Between Batman and Bruce Wayne," she said, "there's no room for me."

"Rachel, I chose this life. I can give it up."

She touched his face gently. "You didn't choose this life, Bruce. It was thrust upon you, the way greatness often is. You've given this city hope, and now it's depending on you. We all are. Good-bye, Bruce."

Walking away, Rachel looked toward the house. "What will you do?"

"I'm going to rebuild it," Bruce replied, "just the way it was. Brick for brick."

Rachel smiled as she left. Bruce watched her go. A moment later Alfred walked up beside him. "Just the way it was, sir?" he asked.

"Yes . . . why?" Bruce asked.

"I thought we might take the opportunity to make

some improvements . . . to the foundation."

Bruce smiled. "Could you mean the southeast corner?"

"Precisely, sir," Alfred said.

ELEVEN

That night, Batman received a signal from Gordon. He was on the station house roof in minutes, where he found a police spotlight partially covered by a black bat-shaped stencil.

"Nice," Batman said to Gordon.

"Couldn't find any mob bosses to strap to the light," Gordon said.

"What can I do for you, Sergeant?"

Gordon flicked off the beacon. "It's *Lieutenant* now. Commissioner Loeb had to promote me. You've started something," Gordon said. "Judge Faden is in jail. Bent cops are running scared, there's hope on the streets. . . ." His words hung uncertainly in the air.

"But?" Batman asked.

"But there's a lot of weirdness out there right now. We still haven't picked up Crane or half the inmates of Arkham that he freed—"

"We will. Gotham will return to normal."

"Will it? What about escalation? We start carrying semiautomatics, they buy automatics. We start wearing Kevlar, they buy armor-piercing rounds."

"And?" Batman prodded.

"And . . . you're wearing a mask and jumping off rooftops." Gordon pulled a clear plastic evidence bag from his pocket. "Take this guy. Armed robbery, double homicide. He's got a taste for theatrics, like you. Leaves a calling card."

He handed Batman the bag. Inside was a playing card. A joker.

"I'll look into it," Batman said.

As Batman dropped from the rooftop, gliding on the night wind, Lieutenant Gordon smiled.

TWELVE

On the street in front of Gotham First National Bank, three burglars checked their equipment. The men were wearing clown masks: white faces, red lips, and bright blue painted smiles.

"We're it?" one clown wondered. "Three guys?" Robbing the bank was a pretty big job for just three burglars.

"There's more on the roof," another clown remarked, pointing up above their heads. Two other men were sliding along a cable toward the rooftop.

Up on the roof, two other clowns were working

to disarm the bank's security system. They were also discussing the mysterious man behind the heist.

"Why do they call him the Joker?" the clown asked as he watched his partner remove screws from an access panel door.

"I heard he wears makeup," the man working the door replied.

"Makeup?" The first clown gave a small laugh.

"Yeah," the handyman said as the panel slid away, revealing a large cluster of wiring and cables. "War paint." His hands moved quickly across the wiring, turning the alarm off. "I'm done here," he announced. The clowns entered the bank.

In the main room, customers screamed. Tellers ducked behind their booths. The masked clowns threatened their hostages.

One clown rushed down to the basement, where another was busy opening a vault. "They wired this thing with five thousand volts," the clown reported. "What kind of bank does that?"

The other clown knew the money they were stealing belonged to organized criminals. "A mob bank," he replied. "Guess the Joker's as crazy as they say."

They filled duffel bags with the mob's money and carried them into the bank's lobby.

At that moment, the back of a yellow school bus rammed through the front window. A final clown loaded all the money bags and climbed into the bus.

Police sirens screamed in the distance, but the last clown remained calm. The man whipped off his clown mask. He was the Joker, Gotham's reigning criminal mastermind.

Lieutenant Gordon stood next to the Bat-Signal. A young detective named Ramirez stepped onto the roof, carrying a cup of coffee. She handed the cup to Gordon.

Gordon gave a half smile. Some people in Gotham were afraid of Batman, scared because he was taking the law into his own hands. The police had standing orders to arrest him on sight. But that was one command Gordon was determined to ignore. He had come to rely on the mysterious Caped Crusader to help the police frighten criminals and keep the city safe.

Everyone at the Major Crimes Unit knew the Bat-Signal was Gordon's way to call Batman when he needed him. No one talked about it, but it was common knowledge that Gordon had developed an odd sort of friendship with Batman. Out of respect for Lieutenant Gordon, no one on his team of officers was really trying to discover Batman's true identity.

"Hasn't shown up?" Ramirez asked, looking at the bat in the sky.

Gordon downed the last of his coffee. "Often doesn't." He crumpled up his cup. "But I like reminding everybody that he's out there."

"Why wouldn't he come?" Detective Ramirez wondered aloud.

"Hopefully," Gordon replied as he flipped the off switch, plunging the sky into complete darkness, "because he's busy."

Meanwhile, two black SUVs and an unmarked white van pulled onto the top floor of a parking garage. A large man climbed out of one of the SUVs. He was a Russian mobster known simply as the Chechen.

The Chechen's bodyguard looked around the parking garage nervously. "What if *he* shows up?" the man asked his boss.

"That's why we bring dogs," the Chechen replied,

speaking to his guard in Russian. "My dogs will take care of the Batman."

The bodyguard opened the back door of the second SUV. Three enormous rottweilers leaped out onto the pavement, growling ferociously.

While the rest of his men waited in the SUVs, the Chechen slowly walked over to the white van, where the Scarecrow was waiting for him. They had just begun to talk about how Batman was hurting the mob's business when suddenly the Chechen's dogs started barking.

"He's here," the bodyguard said uneasily, searching the darkness for any sign of Batman.

"We're all here," a man's voice called out into the night. Five men in Batman costumes emerged from the shadows.

The Chechen's goons were fast and strong. It only took them a few seconds to capture all five Batman impersonators.

The Scarecrow walked over to the prisoners. Their costumes had been created from black masks and hockey pads. "None of these are the real thing," he reported.

Just then, the Batmobile slammed down onto a row of parked cars.

Wham!

"That's more like it," the Scarecrow said with a nod. "This one's the real deal."

Boom!

The Batmobile's cannons roared into action, surrounding the Chechen's men with blasts of fire. In the chaos, the real Batman dropped onto the top of the Chechen's van from his grapnel hook.

Batman fought swiftly. It wasn't long before the Chechen called back his dogs and fled. The Scarecrow, too, ran off and disappeared.

Batman freed the imposters and told them to leave. He wished they would stop trying to help him. He didn't have the time to continually rescue weak imitators.

THIRTEEN

Lieutenant Gordon surveyed the damage at Gotham First National Bank. Officers from MCU were interviewing witnesses, trying to reconstruct what had happened.

Detective Ramirez approached Gordon as he considered the scene.

"He can't resist showing his face," she told her boss, handing him a series of grainy photographs taken by the bank's security cameras.

Gordon flipped through the images. Even without

the rubber mask, the thief still had the appearance of a circus clown—white pancake makeup, stringy green hair, and a ruby-red smile painted over scarred cheeks.

Gordon paused as Batman shifted in the shadows. Without a word, Gordon handed over the photographs. Batman recognized the villain from other photos that had been taken at smaller heists.

"Him again." Batman handed the pictures back to Gordon, not too concerned.

He wanted Gordon to send cops out into the other banks to confiscate the mob's money, then make arrests. Taking down the mob was part of Batman's grand plan to return Gotham to her glory as a safe city.

Gordon also wanted the mob brought to its knees, but he had another pressing concern. "What about this Joker guy?" he asked.

"One man or the entire mob?" Batman asked. "He can wait."

With a nod, Gordon began to talk out his plan of action. He wanted to organize a simultaneous bust on all of the mob banks. "We'll have to hit all banks simultaneously. SWAT teams. Backup. When the new DA gets wind of this, he'll want in."

Harvey Dent was the newly elected district attorney. He'd come from Internal Affairs, where he'd spent his days ferreting out corrupt cops, but that was all Batman knew about the man. "Do you trust him?" Batman asked Gordon.

"It would be hard to keep him out," Gordon replied. "He's as stubborn as you."

With a smile, Lieutenant Gordon looked up, but the place where Batman had been standing was now empty.

"It'll be nice when Wayne Manor's rebuilt and you can swap not sleeping in a penthouse for not sleeping in a mansion," Alfred remarked as he stepped into the artificial light of the Bat-Bunker.

Since the fire, Bruce had lived in a luxury penthouse and had a secret lair within city limits. In the center of the low-ceilinged chamber was the Batmobile. Behind the car, Bruce had set up machines that completely covered one wall: 3-D printers, TV screens, and computers.

Images flickered across two of the screens: closed-circuit TV news footage of the bank robbery at Gotham National on one and a live interview with Harvey Dent on another.

Bruce Wayne was sitting between the screens, his eyes periodically shifting from one to the other.

"Things are improving. Look at the new district attorney," Alfred commented, following Bruce's gaze as it settled on Dent.

"I am," Bruce replied. "Closely. I need to know if he can be trusted."

With the press of a button on a nearby control panel, more images appeared on other screens. Bruce had clearly been following the man for some time. There were videos of the district attorney at a meeting. Campaigning. Helping a woman out of a cab. There was no mistaking the young woman in the scene; Harvey Dent was escorting Rachel Dawes about town.

As Rachel and Dent disappeared into a restaurant, Alfred gave Bruce a questioning look. "Are you interested in his character . . . or his social circle?"

"Who Rachel spends her time with is her business," Bruce said.

Alfred handed Bruce a cup of coffee. "Know your limits, Master Wayne," he warned.

Bruce stared into the steaming brew. "Batman has no limits."

"Ah, but you do, sir," Alfred replied.

"I can't afford to know them," Bruce said.

There was a touch of concern in Alfred's voice as he asked, "What happens the day you find out?"

Bruce turned fully away from his screens and monitors to look at Alfred. "We all know how much you like to say 'I told you so.'"

"That day, Master Wayne, even I won't want to." Alfred headed back to the elevator, muttering under his breath as he pressed the button to take him back up.

FOURTEEN

With Carmine Falcone gone, Sal Maroni was now Gotham's mob boss. Harvey Dent had called one of Maroni's goons into court to testify against him. When Rachel asked her new boss if she could question the witness on the stand, Dent pulled a large silver dollar out of his pocket.

"You're flipping coins to see who leads?" Rachel asked.

Dent smiled fondly at her. "It's my father's lucky coin. As I recall, it got me my first date with you."

He flipped his coin into the air. Heads, he'd take on

the witness. Tails, Rachel would ask the questions.

The coin spun. Rachel didn't see anything funny about using a coin to make an important decision. "I'm serious, Harvey," she told him. "You don't leave things like this to chance."

He caught the dollar and pressed it into the back of his left hand. Heads.

"I don't. I make my own luck." Dent tucked his coin back into his pocket and stepped up to the stand.

A bullet whizzed right by the DA's ear. Harvey Dent bravely stepped forward and snagged the witness's gun in a single, quick, smooth move.

The police removed the criminal. Dent was not fazed.

"Why don't we take the rest of the day off?" Rachel asked.

"Can't," Dent replied, stalling her hands by placing his own over them. "I dragged the head of the Major Crimes Unit down here."

"Jim Gordon?" Rachel asked. "He's a friend," she told Harvey. She added, "Try to be nice." Rachel knew the relationship between Lieutenant Gordon and Dent was strained. Before he became her boss, Dent worked to

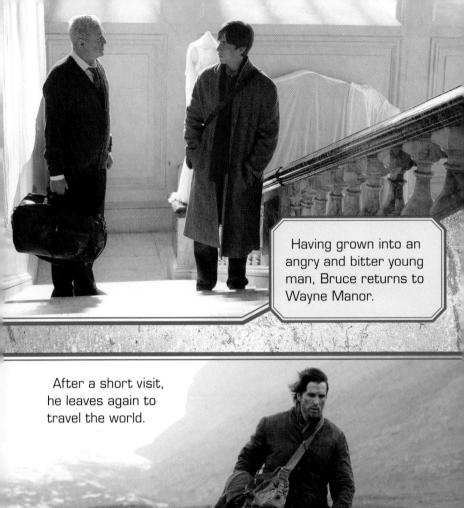

Having grown into an angry and bitter young man, Bruce returns to Wayne Manor.

After a short visit, he leaves again to travel the world.

Bruce trains with the League of Shadows and becomes a skilled warrior with the help of his teacher, Henri Ducard.

Having completed his training, Bruce returns to Gotham.

There Dr. Crane, director of Arkham Asylum, moonlights as the evil Scarecrow.

Lucius Fox provides Bruce with all the tools he needs to protect Gotham against attacks from all entities.

Bruce becomes Batman.

He soon discovers that Dr. Crane is working for the League of Shadows.

Lieutenant Gordon uses the Bat-Signal to call for Batman's help.

Batman races to action in the Batmobile.

Men with clown masks rob Gotham First National Bank.

Harvey Dent and Rachel Dawes fight injustice.

The Joker is Gotham's newest criminal mastermind.

Batman interrogates him to find out where he's hiding Dent and Rachel.

The Bat-Pod gives Batman the ability to weave in and out of traffic. Protecting Gotham is a dangerous job.

bring down dirty cops. His job didn't make him many friends on the police force.

Dent knew Gordon was getting help with these mob busts. "I want to meet *him*," Dent told Gordon.

Gordon looked blankly at the DA as if he didn't know who Dent was talking about.

"Save it, Gordon." Dent knew who'd been working with him. "When can I meet *him*?"

Gordon snidely remarked, "Official policy is to arrest the vigilante known as Batman on sight." It was, after all, Harvey Dent's own rule.

Dent battled back, verbally attacking Gordon's leadership of the Major Crimes Unit. "I don't like that you've got your own 'special' unit, and I don't like that it's full of cops I investigated at Internal Affairs."

Deep down, Gordon knew that Dent was probably right. There might be a couple of bad cops in his ranks, but there wasn't a whole lot he could do about it. "If I didn't work with cops you'd investigated while you were making your name at Internal Affairs," Gordon told Dent, "I'd be working alone. I have to do the best I can with what I have."

Gordon moved on to the business at hand. "I need those search warrants for my ongoing investigation."

"You want me to back warrants for five banks without telling me who we are after?"

"In this town, the fewer people who know about something, the safer the operation," Gordon explained. "I can give you the names of the banks."

"Well, that's a start." Dent pulled some papers from a drawer. "I'll get you your warrants. But I want your trust." He looked hard at Gordon.

Lieutenant Gordon headed to the door. "You don't have to sell me, Dent. We all know you're Gotham's white knight."

Dent grinned. "I hear they have a different nickname for me down at MCU."

Not a very nice one, Gordon thought to himself. But to Dent he simply smiled.

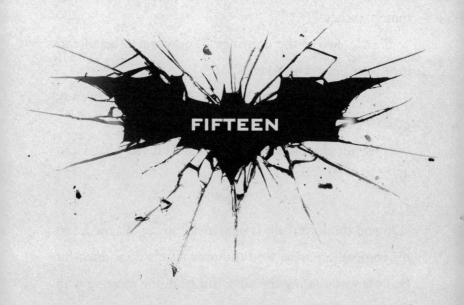

FIFTEEN

It had been a long day. Lucius Fox, now CEO of
Wayne Enterprises, led a meeting with Chairman Lau,
a businessman from China and head of LSI Holdings.
When Lau left the room, though, Bruce immediately
instructed Fox to investigate him and his business.

Changing subjects, Bruce told Fox, "I need a new
suit."

Looking him over, Fox commented, "Three buttons
is a little nineties."

Bruce straightened his tie. "I'm not talking about

fashion, Mr. Fox, so much as function." He pulled out some sketches.

Fox looked at the drawings. "You want to be able to turn your head?" he asked.

"Sure would make backing out of the driveway easier." Bruce smiled.

Fox put the pages in his pocket. "I'll see what I can do."

"Do you think this suit is outdated?" Bruce Wayne asked his companion as he held the restaurant's door open for her. He was wearing the same suit from the meeting with Lau earlier in the day.

She glanced at him and shrugged. She didn't know much about fashion. She also didn't know that good food wasn't the only reason they'd come to this particular restaurant tonight. Bruce knew that Rachel was there with Harvey Dent. Pretending like it was an accidental encounter, he approached the table where Rachel and Dent were reviewing their menus.

"Rachel." Bruce leaned over to kiss her briefly on the cheek. "Fancy that."

Bruce introduced his companion, forcing Rachel

to introduce her date as well. This was the reason he'd come, Bruce reminded himself. He needed to meet Dent.

"The infamous Bruce Wayne." Dent rose to shake hands. "Rachel's told me everything about you."

Bruce couldn't help responding with a smile. "I certainly hope not."

Harvey and Bruce talked about Dent's personal mission to clean up Gotham City. Bruce was impressed by the man's passion.

"I guess you either die a hero or you live long enough to see yourself become the villain," Dent told Bruce. "Look, whoever this Batman is, he doesn't want to spend the rest of his life doing this. How could he? Batman's looking for someone else to take up his mantle."

Bruce's date jumped into the conversation. "Someone like you, maybe, Mr. Dent?"

Dent leaned back in his chair. "Maybe," he replied. "If I'm up to it."

Bruce liked Dent's response. He had begun to consider the possibility that Batman could pass the job of cleaning up Gotham to someone else. If Harvey Dent was going to take on that role, Bruce knew he'd need to secure the man's position as DA.

New elections weren't for another three years, but he could get Harvey the money he'd need to win that election and any others he might have in his future. Bruce offered to have a party for Harvey, a fundraiser. "After an evening with my friends," Bruce explained, "you'll never need another."

It was an invitation Harvey Dent could not refuse.

Across town, some of Gotham's biggest criminals were meeting in a secret conference room. The Chechen, Sal Maroni, and a muscular gangster named Gambol were sitting around a table. On a video monitor was Chairman Lau. He was addressing the group live from a secret location.

"As you are all aware," Lau told the gangsters, "one of our deposits was stolen. A relatively small amount—sixty-eight million dollars."

"Who took it?" the Chechen demanded.

Sal Maroni knew the answer. "The Joker is a two-bit whack job, wears a cheap purple suit and makeup. He's not the problem. He's a nobody."

Lau agreed. "We need to move the money somewhere safe. I believe Hong Kong is our best option."

The gangsters protested. No one wanted the mob's money to leave Gotham. It was *their* money. The men began to argue, unable to decide what to do next, when a roar of laughter filled the room.

The Joker stepped from a dark corner. "Moving your money to Hong Kong won't stop Batman. He has no jurisdiction." The Joker said that there was only one way to protect the mob's money. "Kill the Batman."

"If it's so easy, why haven't you done it already?" Sal Maroni asked. The mobsters in the room began to snicker.

The Joker told the men he would happily do it for them. Only he wanted to be paid for the job. He'd already stolen some of their money. He wanted more.

They refused.

"Let me know when you change your mind," the Joker said, before strolling casually out of the room.

When he was gone, Maroni turned to the screen with Lau. "How soon can you move the money?"

Lau smiled. "I already have." The camera pulled out to reveal that Lau was sitting on an airplane. With the rumble of an engine, the plane lifted off.

The Bat-Signal illuminated the evening sky. Batman landed softly on the roof of the MCU. He expected to find Lieutenant Gordon there. He wanted to hear what the police knew about Chairman Lau. But the man who faced Batman was not Gordon; instead it was Harvey Dent.

"You're a hard man to reach," Dent said as he stepped fully into the light of the Bat-Signal.

The rooftop door suddenly swung open with a resounding crash. Gordon burst onto the roof. He was not happy to discover that Dent had used the Bat-Signal.

"Lau's halfway to Hong Kong," Dent told Gordon. "If you'd only asked, I could have taken his passport. I told you to keep me in the loop."

Gordon responded, "Yeah? Last time your office got involved, we had trouble. There's a leak. . . ."

Dent was offended. "My office? You're sitting down there with scum like Detectives Wuertz and Ramirez . . ."

His voice trailed off as Batman stepped closer to the two men. Now was not the time to argue about whether Gordon had a couple of crooked cops on his team.

Dent told Batman, "We need Lau back."

Batman considered the situation. "If I get him to you, can you get him to talk?"

Dent nodded confidently. "I'll get him to sing."

Gordon piped in. "If we're going after the mob's life savings, things will get ugly." It was a subtle warning to Dent that he was in danger.

"I knew the risks when I took this job, Lieutenant," Dent said firmly. "Same as you." Then, looking back toward Batman, Dent asked, "How will you get him back, anyway?" But Batman had already disappeared.

Gordon smirked and said with a shrug, "He does that."

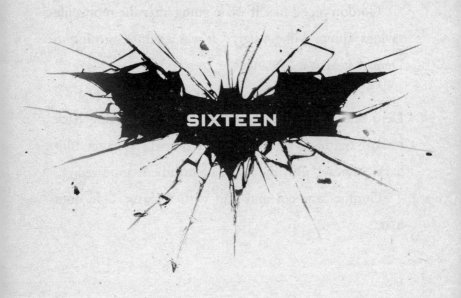

SIXTEEN

In the Applied Sciences lab, Fox was hard at work redesigning the new suit Bruce had requested.

Fox explained how this Batsuit was made. "You'll be lighter, faster, more agile." Fox paused. "Now, there's a trade-off. The spread of the plates gives you weak spots."

"We wouldn't want things getting too easy, would we?" This suit, flaws and all, was exactly what he'd been hoping for.

Bruce put his arm on Fox's shoulder. "I'm sure you've always wanted to go to Hong Kong." He showed

Fox a detailed plan for their trip to find and bring back Chairman Lau. To make the plan work, the first thing they needed was a very special kind of airplane.

Fox knew exactly where to get one.

In Hong Kong, shortly before day break, Batman crouched on the rooftop of a building directly across from LSI Holdings. The new Batsuit moved comfortably, and the redesigned cowl allowed him the freedom to turn his head with greater ease.

Batman pulled two black boxes from his Utility Belt and snapped them together to create a high-powered, scope-like rifle.

Slightly below where he stood was Chairman Lau's window. Batman fired four times. With each silenced explosion, a sticky bomb attached to the glass of the LSI building. Moving quickly, Batman leaped into the vast space between the two buildings and floated toward a large window. He crashed through the glass.

Lau's office door was locked. Batman kicked in the door and swooped down on Chairman Lau. In a lightning-fast move, Batman attached a small pack to Lau's back, and then, just as he'd planned, the timers on

Batman's four sticky bombs ticked down to zero.

The police burst into the office just as the wall and ceiling behind Lau and Batman exploded. Batman quickly pulled the rip cord on Lau's pack. A weather balloon emerged from the pack, filling itself with helium. The balloon floated gently two hundred feet up, attached to Lau by a thin thread of high-test nylon.

A low rumble filled the room. The rumble grew louder and louder until the thread from Batman's weather-balloon pack was caught in the nose of a massive, soaring aircraft.

Lau and Batman were yanked from the building and carried off into the glowing orange-and-yellow sunrise.

A few days later, Lieutenant Gordon was in his office looking through case files when Detective Ramirez rushed in.

"You're gonna want to see this," she told Gordon.

He followed her down the stairs and out the front door.

Chairman Lau was sitting on the ground, tied up and gagged. A sign taped to his chest read: *Please deliver to Lieutenant Gordon.*

A few paces away, the media was interviewing Harvey Dent about Lau's miraculous reappearance.

"By taking Lau out of Hong Kong, the Chinese government claims its international rights have been broken." The reporter thrust his microphone into Dent's face. "How do you respond?"

"I don't know about Mr. Lau's travel arrangements," Dent said with a small laugh. "But I'm sure glad he's back."

The DA had a plan. If Lau would give them damaging information about the mob, he could charge all of Gotham's mobsters as one criminal. They would all go down together.

Lau made a deal with Harvey Dent. In exchange for information, Lau would be given exactly what he wanted: immunity, protection, and a chartered plane back to Hong Kong. They also agreed that Lau would stay at MCU, where Gordon could keep an eye on him, rather than at the county jail.

Within the hour, SWAT teams were dispatched throughout Gotham City. The police nabbed 549 of the mob's nastiest thugs, including Sal Maroni.

The criminals arrived in overcrowded buses at Gotham Municipal Court.

Paperwork was piled on Judge Surillo's desk in thick

stacks. With more than five hundred defendants, people were squeezed into every nook and cranny of the courtroom.

She read the charges. "Eight hundred forty-nine counts racketeering. Two hundred forty-six counts fraud. Eighty-seven counts conspiracy murder—" A playing card slid out from between two documents—a joker.

Judge Surillo set the card aside and began the trial.

"The public likes you, Dent," Mayor Garcia told the DA. They were in city hall, across the street from Judge Surillo's chaotic courtroom. "That's the only reason this might fly."

"They're all coming after you, now," he warned. "Not just the mob. Politicians, journalists, cops—anyone whose wallet is about to get lighter without the mob's money in the hidden lining." Dent didn't blink against the mayor's unwavering stare. "Are you up to it?"

Dent was ready for anything that might come at him.

"You better be. If they get anything on you . . . those criminals will be back on the streets."

The mayor stepped over to the window and looked outside, adding softly, "Followed swiftly by you and me—"

Bang!

A dark shape cracked the glass in front of the mayor's office.

"It's Batman." Dent stared at the limp body that had hit the mayor's window. The body was hanging by its neck from the municipal flagpole, cape loosely billowing in the wind.

Dent rushed outside to get a closer look.

It wasn't Batman after all, but an imposter. A joker was pinned to the imitation Batsuit.

Dent stood by as Lieutenant Gordon read the handwritten note on the playing card aloud: "Will the real Batman please reveal himself?"

In Bruce Wayne's plush penthouse, Alfred was busy overseeing the decorations for the Dent fundraiser.

"How's it going?" Bruce asked Alfred.

"I think your fundraiser will be a great success, sir," Alfred said with a smile.

Across the bottom of the screen, in a bright bold font, read the words IS BATMAN DEAD?

An image of a fake Batman filled the screen.

"Police have released video footage found concealed on the body," the anchor reported as the tape began to roll.

Looking straight at the camera, the Joker declared, "You want order in Gotham? Batman has to go." He leaned in to the screen, his disturbingly comical face filling the picture. "Batman must take off his mask and turn himself in. Every day he doesn't, people will die. Starting tonight. I am a man of my word."

Bruce clicked off the TV and sank back into his couch. He needed a plan.

Detective Ramirez was in a meeting with Lieutenant Gordon. They'd sent the joker card to the lab to check for fingerprints. The results were in.

"There are three. They belong to Judge Surillo, Harvey Dent, and Commissioner Loeb," Ramirez reported.

Gordon realized that the matches were for the Joker's future victims. He barked orders at Ramirez. "Get a unit to Surillo's house. Tell Detective Wuertz to find Dent. Get them both into protective custody." He surveyed the police working quietly at their desks in MCU. It was the calm before the storm. "Where's the commissioner?"

"City hall."

Gordon nodded at Ramirez. "Seal the building. No one in or out till I get there."

Judge Surillo got into her car. Two men in police uniforms had told her that Gordon wanted her to get safely out of town. Trusting the officers, Surillo started the engine. A second later, her car exploded, heaving upward in a massive fireball.

From the wreckage, burning playing cards fluttered onto the street.

Jokers.

Lieutenant Gordon rushed to Commissioner Loeb. "I'm sorry, sir. We believe the Joker has made a threat against your life," he said.

"Take my word for it: The police commissioner earns a lot of threats. I found the appropriate response to these situations a long time ago."

Gordon felt that Loeb was being much too calm about the situation. "Sir," he explained, "the joker card had your fingerprint on it."

"How'd they get my print?" Loeb asked before taking a drink from the glass on his desk.

"Somebody with access to your house or office must've lifted it off a tissue or a glass," Gordon said, considering the possibilities. With sudden realization, Gordon shouted, "Wait!"

Loeb was already choking. He stumbled back, grasping at his throat, gasping for air. Liquid spilled across the desk, and within seconds it was smoking, eating its way through the wood, biting into the metal beneath.

"Get a medic!" Gordon shouted, even though he knew it was too late.

Gordon then called Detective Wuertz and ordered him to find Harvey Dent. Quickly.

Dent was next on the Joker's list.

SEVENTEEN

Bruce arrived late to the Dent fundraiser, making a grand entrance by helicopter. "I'm so glad you started without me!" He held up a copy of Dent's campaign poster and read the text: "I believe in Harvey Dent." The poster had an American flag down the center, overlaid with a picture of Harvey.

"Nice slogan, Harvey," Bruce said. Then he addressed the crowd: "I started paying attention to Harvey too, and kept my eye on the things he's been doing as our new DA, and you know what?" Bruce pointed a finger at himself. "Now *I* believe in Harvey Dent." A cheer rose from the crowd.

Bruce rode the wave of applause and continued. "On his watch, Gotham feels a little safer. A little more optimistic. So," he told his friends, "get out your checkbooks, and let's make sure that he stays right where all of Gotham wants him!" Alfred passed Bruce a glass, which he raised high in a toast. "To the face of Gotham's bright future—Harvey Dent."

Nodding graciously, Dent thanked his host.

Having thrown his support behind the one man good enough to stop crime in Gotham, Bruce went outside to his patio.

Rachel joined him.

"Rachel." He struggled to tell her how he felt. "The day you once told me about, the day when Gotham no longer needs Batman—it's coming."

Gotham needed Batman, and he could not give up the role until someone else came along to be Gotham's hero.

"It's happening now," Bruce said excitedly. "Harvey can be the hero. He locked up half the city's criminals, and he did it without wearing a mask. Gotham needs a champion with a face."

"You can't ask me to wait . . . ," Rachel began. There was a noise at the door.

Unaware of what he was interrupting, Dent came out onto the balcony. "You sure can throw a party, Wayne. Thanks again." He shook Bruce's hand vigorously. "Mind if I borrow Rachel?"

Rachel glanced over her shoulder at Bruce as Dent led her back into the bustle of the party.

Bruce wished things were different. He'd happily give up being Batman to be with Rachel. That was his plan. He hoped he wasn't too late.

Dent took Rachel into the kitchen. He said, "Facing death makes you think about what you couldn't stand losing. And who you want to spend the rest of your life with."

"The rest of your life, huh?" Rachel's heart sped up. She hadn't expected to have this conversation with Harvey. Not tonight. "Marriage is a pretty big commitment."

Harvey smiled and took both her hands in his. "What's your answer?"

As she considered his proposal, Bruce entered the kitchen. Sneaking up behind Harvey, Bruce grabbed him in a sleeper hold, and he slumped to the floor.

"What are you doing?" Rachel demanded.

"They've come for him." Bruce quickly filled her in. "I just got a call. The Joker's men got to Judge Surillo *and* Commissioner Loeb."

At that moment, guests at the party began to scream.

Bruce stuffed Harvey into a closet. "Stay hidden," he warned Rachel as he slipped out the kitchen door.

The Joker moved through the party, his fake smile frightening the guests.

"Where is Harvey Dent?"

No one answered. Joker threatened a man and his wife with a knife.

Rachel could not stay hidden. "Stop!" She stepped boldly into the room.

"Hello, beautiful," Joker greeted Rachel, grabbing her arm and pulling her close. "You must be Harvey's squeeze. You look nervous. It's the scars, isn't it?"

Rachel didn't respond. She kept her gaze steady and refused to show him fear.

When he stepped slightly back, she slugged him hard in the stomach.

The Joker touched the sore spot and mocked, "A little fight in you. I like that."

"Then you're going to love me!" Batman said as he pounced, catching the Joker with a powerful blow. The villain fell backward, away from Rachel.

As Batman approached, the Joker kicked at him with a knife that was hidden in his shoe. The blade caught Batman between the armored plates of his Batsuit, right in the vulnerable spot Fox had warned him about.

Ignoring his own pain, Batman leaped toward the Joker, grabbing him around the waist and hurling him across the room.

The Joker got to his feet and grabbed Rachel once again. "Just take off your mask and show us who you are."

Rachel shook her head at Batman.

"Fine, then," the Joker said, raising the stakes. He pulled out a shotgun and blasted a pane of glass in the window next to him. Dragging Rachel over to the hole, Joker dangled her out the window.

"Let her go." Batman's voice was steady and serious.

"Very poor choice of words." The Joker laughed as he opened his fist.

Rachel was falling. No one could survive the long drop from Wayne's penthouse to the pavement below.

Swoosh!

Batman leaped out the window after her, wrapping his arms around her. By activating the fabric of his cape, he managed to slow their descent, but not enough to prevent a crash.

Slam!

Batman enveloped Rachel in his cape as together they smashed into the hood of a taxi.

The driver yelped as they rolled off the hood, down the windshield, and onto the pavement. They were scraped and bruised, but alive.

The Joker escaped the party, and Dent was safe.

For now.

EIGHTEEN

Bruce was deeply troubled by what had happened to Judge Surillo and Commissioner Loeb. He didn't want more people to get hurt because of him.

Bruce looked at his Batsuit, considering the problem. "Criminals aren't complicated, Alfred. We just have to figure out what this Joker person is after."

Alfred shook his head. "Respectfully, Master Wayne, perhaps this is a man you don't fully understand." Alfred told Bruce that not every criminal has a reason for his violence. "Some men aren't looking for anything logical, like money. They can't be bought, bullied, reasoned with, or negotiated with." Alfred's voice dropped to a whisper. "Some men just want to watch the world burn."

Hours before the funeral for Commissioner Loeb was about to begin, Gordon saw a campaign poster for Mayor Garcia defaced with a crazy clown grin and "ha, ha, ha." Lieutenant Gordon realized the Joker was adding to his list of victims.

Bruce Wayne went to the funeral, hoping he could protect both men. He scanned the buildings, noting police snipers on every rooftop. SWAT team members surrounded the stage. After the mayor spoke, an honor guard was going to fire bullets into the air to salute the late commissioner.

Bruce looked at each police officer and each SWAT team member. He was checking out every person in the guard one by one—when he found the Joker. The permanent smile on his face gave him away.

The service began, and Bruce struggled to get through the crowd. He didn't make it before the speeches ended. The honor guard raised their weapons, and when it was time, the Joker fired not at the sky, but directly at the mayor. Gordon dived, saving the mayor by taking the bullet himself.

The crowd screamed. People ran in every direction. From where he'd been sitting on the stage, Harvey Dent had seen a SWAT team member shoot one of the Joker's men in the leg. Dent knew the man was now in the back of an ambulance. Dent wanted to interview him before they went to the hospital.

Distracting the ambulance driver, Dent leaped into the front seat and drove the Joker's thug to an abandoned building.

It took only a few minutes of questioning for Dent to get his answer. The Joker's next target was Rachel.

When Rachel answered Harvey's desperate call, she was at the Major Crimes Unit. Cops and eyewitnesses were crammed in every available chair and interview space. "Harvey Dent, where are you?" Rachel asked.

Dent didn't answer the question. "Where are you?"

She was annoyed. "I'm where you should be, at Major Crimes, trying to sort through all the—"

He cut her off. "Rachel, listen to me, you're not safe there."

She didn't understand. "This is Gordon's unit, Harvey."

"Gordon's gone, Rachel," Dent said. "I just heard that the Joker's named you next." He continued, "Rachel, I can't let anything happen to you. I love you too much. Is there anyone in the city we can trust?"

"Bruce. We can trust Bruce Wayne." Her voice was strong and certain.

"OK. Don't tell anyone where you're going. I'll find you at his penthouse."

After hanging up, Dent went back to questioning the injured gunman. He wanted to know the Joker's true identity.

Batman appeared, interrupting the interrogation.

Dent told Batman, "The Joker got Gordon and Loeb, and now he's going to get Rachel!"

Batman calmly replied, "You're the symbol of hope that I could never be. Your stand against organized crime is the first legitimate ray of light in Gotham for decades. If anyone saw this"—he indicated the thug bound to the chair, cowering in fear—"everything would be undone;

all the criminals you got off the streets would be released. And Jim Gordon would have died for nothing."

Batman explained to Dent what he needed to do. "You're going to call a press conference. Tomorrow morning."

"Why?" Dent asked.

"No one else will die because of me," Batman said. "Gotham is in your hands now."

"You can't! You can't give in!" Dent shouted, but his words merely echoed off the walls in the abandoned basement. Once again, Batman had disappeared like a shadow in the night.

Rachel went to Bruce's penthouse. When Bruce got home, Rachel stood with him outside on the balcony.

"Harvey just called," she said. "He says Batman's going to turn himself in."

"I have no choice," he sighed.

"You honestly think it's going to stop the Joker?" Rachel stared at him as if he'd lost his mind.

Bruce turned to look at her. "Perhaps not, but I've got enough blood on my hands. I've seen, now, what I would have to become to stop men like him." He paused.

"You once told me that if the day came when I was finished"—Bruce took a step closer to Rachel—"we'd be together."

"Bruce, don't make me your one hope for a normal life."

He pulled her into his arms. "Did you mean it?" he asked very simply.

"Yes," Rachel replied before stepping away. But she knew that things would never be normal. She couldn't marry Bruce, no matter how much she wanted to. She needed to marry Harvey Dent. Let Gotham have Batman. It was the right thing to do. For everyone.

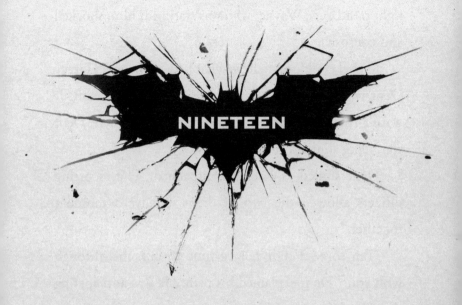

NINETEEN

"Ladies and gentlemen," Harvey Dent began the press conference, "thank you for coming. The Joker's killings will now come to an end, because Batman has offered to turn himself in."

"So where is he?" a reporter called out.

Bruce Wayne began to step forward when Dent turned to the officers and said, "Take the Batman into custody." Dent offered up his own wrists to the officers. "I am the Batman."

Cuffed, head held high, Harvey Dent allowed himself

to be ushered out of the chaotic pressroom. He walked right past Bruce Wayne, who was staring at him, shocked and confused.

Rachel could not believe what had happened! Harvey Dent was being arrested for claiming to be Batman. It wasn't true. She hurried to the pressroom, where Dent was being shuttled into a police van.

Dent smiled as Rachel approached. The escorting officers allowed the two of them to have a moment together.

"I'm sorry. I didn't have time to talk this through with you." Dent explained his plan. He was anticipating that the Joker would make an attempt to get to him while the police transferred him to Central Holding. "This is the Joker's chance, and when he attacks, Batman will take him down," he told Rachel.

"Don't offer yourself as bait, Harvey," Rachel pleaded. "This is too dangerous."

Dent grinned and, looping his cuffed hands around her neck, pulled her in for a kiss. "I have an idea," he said. Then, pulling back his hands, he reached down into his pocket. Dent pulled out his lucky silver dollar. "Heads, I go through with it."

"This is your life," Rachel chastised him. "You don't leave something like this to chance."

"I'm not." Dent tossed the coin to Rachel. She caught it and opened her hand. It was heads. As the van's doors closed and it slipped into place in a long line of police-car escorts, Rachel turned the coin over in her hand.

Heads on both sides.

Rachel watched the convoy pull away. "You make your own luck," she murmured to herself.

In the rear of the police van, Dent sat with SWAT in full protective gear. When the van began to slow, he knew he'd been right; the Joker was going to attack.

Suddenly, a huge truck smashed into the front of the armored car.

The Joker was hanging out the back door as he fired a rocket launcher at the van.

Blam!

He hit a nearby police car instead. It exploded.

Through the debris, a dark form appeared. It crashed through the blast with a blast of its own.

Batman had arrived.

The Batmobile slammed through traffic, aimed at rescuing Harvey Dent.

The Joker turned, pointed his weapon at Batman, and fired.

A direct hit. The rear of the Batmobile burst into flames and spun out of control. The Batmobile flipped over and over, finally coming to rest in a smoldering heap.

From the wreckage of the Batmobile, the motorcycle-like Bat-Pod shot forward. The sleek vehicle cleared the churning wreckage of the Batmobile and set off after the armored van and the Joker's truck.

When he reached striking distance, Batman fired a harpoon. It caught the truck just below the bumper. Batman zoomed ahead, wrapping the cables attached to the harpoon around a lamppost.

The cable forced the speeding truck to flip end over end. From beneath the twisted metal, the Joker crawled out. He rushed into the road, placing himself directly in the path of the oncoming Bat-Pod.

Batman swerved. The Bat-Pod slipped off the road and slammed at full force into a large brick wall. Batman lay motionless in the street.

The Joker walked over and reached for Batman's black cowl, ready to unmask the injured vigilante. An electric shock shot out from the mask and made him pull back.

As the Joker crouched lower toward Batman, the armored van skidded to a stop by the side of the road. The driver jumped out of the van, weapon raised.

"Got you!" the driver announced, pulling off his SWAT helmet to reveal himself. It was Lieutenant Gordon.

The rear of the van opened, and Harvey Dent came rushing forward. "Back from the dead?"

"I couldn't chance my family's safety."

Dent nodded; respect showed in his eyes.

Gordon shoved the Joker into the back of a waiting squad car and drove off to MCU. Dent rode home with Detective Wuertz.

Batman managed to get on the Bat-Pod and drove away.

The Joker was under arrest.

TWENTY

Barbara Gordon turned off the TV to answer the doorbell. When she saw her husband standing on the stoop, she started to sob.

They held each other a short while before little James came out of his room. "Did Batman save you, Dad?" James Gordon Jr. asked, rushing into his father's open arms.

Gordon lifted his son tenderly and said, "Actually, this time I saved him."

The phone rang, and Barbara went to answer it.

"It's for you," she said, handing her husband the phone. "*Commissioner* Gordon."

Jim grinned as he reached for the phone, knowing that with Loeb gone, he was being promoted to the head of Gotham's police department.

Gordon moved through a room of detectives crowded in the observation room. They all wanted to talk to him and congratulate him.

It took a few more minutes than he'd wanted, but when he finally reached the holding cell, he knew exactly what he needed to do. There was a new problem, and he was certain that the Joker was involved.

He stormed into the room and told the Joker, "Harvey Dent never made it home."

"Of course not," the Joker replied.

Gordon surveyed the man's pasty white makeup and snarled purple jacket. His detectives had told him they were having difficulty identifying who the Joker really was. But his identity wasn't Gordon's primary concern; finding Dent was.

"What have you done with him?"

The Joker laughed. "Me? I was right here. Who did

you leave him with? Your people? Assuming of course they are *your* people. . . ."

"Where is he?" Gordon asked, his patience fraying.

Leaning back in the cold metal chair, the Joker looked at his wrist, as if he were checking a watch. "What time is it?" he asked.

"What difference does that make?" Gordon asked.

The new commissioner walked out, intentionally leaving the room unguarded.

Flick!

The overhead lights came on. "Where's Dent?" Batman's voice exploded in the small, closed room.

The Joker started laughing.

Batman asked another question: "Why do you want to kill me?"

Now the Joker was laughing so hard it sounded like crying. "Kill you? I don't want to kill you. What would I do without you? Go back to ripping off mob dealers? No, you . . ." He pointed at Batman. "You. Complete. Me."

Batman shook his head. "You're garbage who kills for money."

The Joker replied, "We're exactly the same. And as

118

soon as the chips are down, people will turn against you. To them, you are a freak like me. They need you right now. But as soon as they don't, they'll cast you out like a leper."

"I'm not a monster," Batman countered. "I'm just ahead of the curve." With that, Batman grabbed the Joker and pulled him upright. "Where's Dent?" In one swing he tossed the Joker against the wall.

The Joker didn't even groan. Instead he picked himself up, saying, "You live by society's rules, and you think they'll save your soul."

"I only have one rule." Batman grabbed the Joker by his neck. "No one dies by my hand."

"Tonight you're going to break your one rule," the Joker replied.

Tightening his grip on the Joker's throat, Batman leaned in closer to his face. "I'm considering it."

The Joker choked out his next sentence. "There are just minutes left, so you'll have to play my little game if you want to save"—he paused a beat—"one of them."

"Them?" Batman realized that the Joker had Dent *and* Rachel!

"Where are they?" Batman bellowed.

"You will now choose one life over the other." The Joker grinned as he laid out the options. "Dent is at Two-fifty Fifty-second Boulevard, and Rachel is on Avenue X at Cicero." The Joker raised his eyebrows, challenging Batman to pick one.

Batman could only stare at the Joker, furious at this terrible game he was playing.

Rachel or Harvey Dent. Who would he save?

Batman gave the Joker one last swift kick in the side and hurried out into the night.

Soon after, the Joker made his one permitted phone call. It was linked to a cell phone that triggered a bomb in the basement of MCU.

The Joker was now free.

Rachel Dawes was alone in an abandoned warehouse. She was tied to a chair, scared, but hopeful that she would soon be rescued.

"Can anyone hear me?" she called out into the empty space.

"Rachel, is that you?" It was Dent. Rachel struggled against the ropes that were holding her. She couldn't move. Looking around, squinting in the blackness, she spotted the source of the voice. A small speaker was on the ground. Rachel discovered something else, too. Behind the speaker stood metal barrels hooked to a car battery and a clock. The timer read five minutes.

Rachel started to cry.

Dent spoke softly, comforting her. "It's OK, Rachel. Everything's going to be just fine."

Harvey Dent was also tied to a chair, across town from Rachel. He shoved his feet on the ground, hard and firm. His chair turned slightly.

Slam.

Now he could see his surroundings better.

He saw metal barrels, a car battery, and a timer that read three-fifteen. Counting down.

Dent dragged his chair, inches at a time, across the cold cement floor. "Look for something to free yourself," he told Rachel as he struggled to reach the barrels and the battery. He was close when his chair suddenly caught a ridge in the floor, and Harvey Dent toppled over, slamming into a barrel and spilling gasoline onto the floor.

"Harvey? What's happening?" Rachel called out.

Harvey couldn't move. The left side of his face was pressed into the floor, drenched in gas. . . .

"They said only one of us was going to make it. They'd let our friends choose." Rachel sighed. "Harvey," she said, as the seconds clicked away, "I want you to know something."

Dent was choking on fuel. "They're coming for you, Rachel," he assured her. "It's OK. Everything's going to be just fine."

Ten seconds remained.

"I don't want to live without you. Because I do have an answer, and my answer is yes," Rachel said.

Wham!

The solid basement door smashed open. With seconds to spare, Batman rushed inside only to find Dent, not Rachel.

The Joker had lied. Batman should have known. Batman was good at games, but his emotions had gotten the better of him and he hadn't thought it through.

Now Batman could only hope Commissioner Gordon had reached Rachel in time.

The counter hit five seconds. Batman grabbed Dent.

"No! Not me!" Dent shrieked. "Why did you come for me?"

Over the loudspeaker Harvey Dent could hear Rachel's last words before the explosion ripped through the warehouse.

Back in his apartment, Bruce had taken off the Batman uniform and had collapsed into a chair. Nothing had gone the way he'd hoped. Rachel was gone. He wanted to give up.

Alfred handed Batman's mask to Bruce, saying, "Gotham needs you."

"Gotham needs its hero," Bruce replied. "And I let the Joker send him to the hospital." Bruce couldn't shake off the images of Harvey Dent being taken away in an ambulance.

"Which is why for now they'll have to do with you." Alfred handed Batman's cowl to Bruce. Reluctantly, Bruce accepted the black mask, searching in its empty eyes for greater meaning.

At Gotham General Hospital, Commissioner Gordon entered Harvey Dent's room.

"I'm sorry about Rachel," Gordon said softly, then waited patiently for Dent to reply. But Dent said nothing. He kept his face turned away. "The doctor says you are in agonizing pain but won't accept medication. That you're refusing skin grafts. . . ."

Dent interrupted Gordon, not commenting on the medication but asking a question instead. "Remember that name you all had for me years ago, when I was at Internal Affairs? What was it, Gordon?"

"Harvey, I can't—" Gordon protested. It wasn't a very nice name.

"Say it!" Dent shrieked. His voice echoed off the walls.

Commissioner Gordon was embarrassed that his team had ever called Harvey Dent names behind his back. "Two-Face," he said softly. "Harvey Two-Face."

Dent turned in his hospital bed, showing Gordon his two faces. His right side was normal, but the left . . . the left side of his face was hideously burned. Gordon gasped.

"Why should I hide who I am?" Dent asked, his voice bitter and scathing.

Gordon took a deep breath and apologized from his heart. "I'm sorry, Harvey."

Harvey Dent would never accept Gordon's apology. "No, you're not," he responded. "Not yet."

TWENTY-ONE

A voice attracted Bruce and Alfred to the TV. "We have with us today a lawyer for a prestigious consultancy. He says he waited as long as he could for the Batman to do the right thing. But now he's taking matters into his own hands. We'll be live at five with the true identity of the Batman—stay with us."

After a short commercial break, the host began taking viewer calls for the lawyer.

An old lady came on the line. "Mr. Reese," she asked. "What's more valuable? One life or a hundred?"

The lawyer didn't hesitate. "I guess it would depend on the life."

But the caller wasn't an old lady at all. It was the Joker. "I'm glad you feel that way. Because I've put a bomb in one of the city's hospitals. It's going off in sixty minutes unless someone kills you. I had a vision of a world without Batman. And it was so . . . boring."

The line went dead.

At MCU, Commissioner Gordon shouted to anyone within hearing range, "Call in every officer! The priority is Gotham General Hospital. Wheel everybody out of that place right now. My hunch is that's where the bomb is."

"Why Gotham General?" Detective Murphy asked.

Gordon took a deep breath. "Because that's where Harvey Dent is."

The police rushed to the hospital to help patients, nurses, and doctors evacuate. They were being loaded onto local school buses to be taken to safe spots throughout the city.

The Joker laughed as he walked slowly through the

empty halls, pressing the large red button on a detonator. Blasts exploded behind him, one after another like the steady beats of a drum. Grinning madly, the Joker strolled out of the hospital and onto one of the crowded school buses.

After igniting one last enormous explosion, he gave a thumbs-up to the bus driver.

The hijacked bus merged into traffic and headed off to the next stop, where the Joker's full day of fun would continue.

During the chaos at the hospital, Harvey Dent walked out and went straight to the warehouse at 250 Fifty-second Boulevard. He would always consider the place Rachel's tomb.

A glitter in the burned-out wreckage caught his eye. Harvey Dent bent low and picked up his silver dollar. On one side, the face had a charred scar across it from the explosion. Dent flipped the coin over in his hand. Ironically, the other side looked as good as new.

As Dent rubbed the coin between his fingers, anger, frustration, and sorrow consumed him until he could no longer think clearly. He would get revenge on those who had failed to save Rachel. He'd get his justice.

Bruce Wayne had secretly been supporting the development of a sonar tracker. The technology allowed Bruce to spy on every cell phone user in the city.

He asked Lucius Fox to monitor the machine and help him locate the Joker.

Fox refused. "Spying on thirty million people wasn't in my job description."

At that moment, the Joker appeared on the computer screens. "What does it take to make you people want to join in the fun?" the Joker asked. "I've got to get you off the bench and into the game. So here it is." His face moved closer to the camera lens. "Come nightfall, this city is mine, and anyone left here plays by my rules. If you don't want to be in the game, get out now."

There were very few ways out of Gotham City. Most people would have to leave by bridges and tunnels. With a sinister laugh, the Joker added, "But the bridge-and-tunnel crowd are in for a surprise." His image faded to static.

With no other options, Fox turned to Batman. "I'll help you this one time."

They agreed that after Batman stopped the Joker, the tracking machine would be destroyed.

TWENTY-TWO

Gothamites were pouring into the streets, anxious to leave, but getting out was complicated. Because of the Joker's threats, the bridges and tunnels were deserted while the bomb squads searched them inch by inch.

Thirty thousand people arrived for eight hundred ferry seats. Commissioner Gordon suggested that the ferries be divided: one for the prisoners from Gotham's jails and one for civilians. Once everyone was loaded, the National Guard told both boats to leave the dock.

Shortly after they moved out, both ferries lost power.

They sat dark and unmoving in the water.

When the pilot on the prisoner ferry went to the engine room, he discovered a bomb. And a remote control.

The captain of the civilian ferry also found a bomb and a remote.

The Joker's voice rang out through speakers on both boats.

"Tonight, you're all going to be part of a social experiment," the Joker announced. "Each of you has a remote to destroy the other ferry. At midnight, I'll destroy all of you. If, however, one of you presses the button before then, I'll let that boat live. You choose." He paused a beat. "Oh, and you might want to decide quickly, because the people on the other boat might not be so noble."

With a laugh, the Joker clicked off the line.

Batman was sitting atop an elevated roadway overlooking Gotham City while Fox monitored the tracker.

In the distance, Batman could see the ferries.

"Fox?" He needed immediate information. "There is something going on with the ferries."

"I'm zeroing in." Fox gave directions as Batman fired up his engine. "Head west."

The Joker was holed up in an apartment tower.

Batman caught up with Gordon on the rooftop of a building across the street from the Joker. Gordon's SWAT leaders had already set up sniper and scope positions. On the penthouse level, Gordon could see the Joker's men.

"We have clear shots on the five clowns. Snipers can take them out, smash the windows," a SWAT leader explained to Gordon. "Then a team rappels in, and another team moves by the stairwells." He indicated on a blueprint map exactly where the stairwells were located. "There will be two or three casualties, max."

Commissioner Gordon didn't hesitate. "Let's do it!"

Batman looked out over the side of the rooftop at the building. "It's not that simple. With the Joker it never is. There's *always* a catch with him." Batman didn't want Gordon to act impulsively. "I need five minutes. Alone." He needed to get himself into the Joker's mind. To figure out . . .

"No." Gordon moved away. "There's no time. We

have clear shots now." The SWAT team took aim. "Dent disappeared from the hospital. I think that Dent's in there. We have to save Dent! *I* have to save Dent!" Gordon turned to his SWAT team leader. "Get ready."

Undeterred by the SWAT team's weapons, Batman leaped in front of them, soaring off the rooftop, opening his cape as he spanned the gulf between the two buildings.

With an exasperated sigh, Gordon told the SWAT team to stand down for two minutes.

Batman was going to face the Joker.

Swoosh!

Batman softly landed against the glass exterior of the building. He took out a canister and sprayed a thin sheet of plastic onto the glass. It hardened instantly.

Crack!

The window silently shattered.

After fighting through the Joker's henchmen, Batman found his primary target.

"You came," the Joker said, turning away from the window as Batman entered the room. He'd been expecting Batman to arrive. "I'm touched." With a whistle and a casual wave of his hand, the Joker called his dogs.

A pack of beasts leaped on Batman, smashing him to the ground.

Batman fought valiantly, rolling over and over as he shook off each dog. Embroiled in battle, Batman never saw Joker's attack coming. From the tip of his clown shoe, a switchblade popped out. Just as Batman tossed off the last of the dogs, Joker kicked his blade into the vulnerable place in Batman's armor. "All the old familiar places," the Joker mocked, reminding Batman of their meeting in Wayne's penthouse, when he'd first discovered that Batman had this weak spot.

Batman recoiled in pain. Angry, evil energy filled the room, and the Joker's attacks became more and more aggressive. With each kick, Batman rolled closer to the glass window and a death drop to the street below.

Crack!

The Joker flung Batman into the glass window. The window's steel frame broke loose. Flinging his arms over his head, Batman protected himself.

Batman grunted as he struggled to hold up the steel

beam while shards of broken glass rained down around him.

"If we don't stop fighting, we're going to miss the fireworks," the Joker remarked, casually stepping onto the steel beam that Batman was supporting with his forearms. "Here we go . . ."

"There won't *be* any fireworks," Batman groaned, struggling to keep the beam from crushing his neck. It was midnight. The ferries were both silent. "What were you hoping to prove? That deep down we're all as ugly as you?"

The Joker looked at the clock on the penthouse wall. Disappointment showed on his face.

"You're alone," Batman told him, with gasping breaths. By refusing to set off the ferry explosions themselves, the citizens of Gotham had proved they wouldn't succumb to pressure.

The Joker bent low over Batman and showed him the dual remote. "Can't really rely on anyone these days." The Joker was ready to destroy both ferries. "You have to do everything yourself." A victorious smile spread across the Joker's face. "You know how I got these scars?"

Batman was still pinned under the steel beam. He

looked up and said, "No." He'd found a way out from under the beam. "But I know how you got this one." Scalloped blades fired out of Batman's gauntlet, nailing the Joker in the chest and arm. Batman managed to grab the remote control as the clown staggered back, slipping off the steel beam and falling toward the street.

Batman fired his grapnel hook at the Joker's leg.

"Augh!" the Joker screamed as he snapped to a stop. Batman hauled him up, back into the shattered building.

"Just couldn't let go of me, could you?" Joker asked with a wink.

"You'll be in a padded cell. *Forever*," Batman said, shaking his head.

"Just wait," the Joker bragged, "until they find out what I did with the best of them. Until they get a good look at the real Harvey Dent, and all the heroic things he's done." The Joker had one more game to play.

Batman hauled the Joker up so they were nose to nose. "What did you do?"

The Joker chuckled, saying, "I took Gotham's white knight. And I brought him down to my level. It wasn't hard—madness is like gravity. All it needs is a little push."

The Joker began to laugh heartily.

Batman turned the Joker over to SWAT and immediately called Gordon.

Strange . . . Gordon didn't answer his phone. When Batman called, Gordon *always* answered his phone.

Batman drew his cape around himself. The night was not over yet.

TWENTY-THREE

Commissioner Gordon didn't see Batman's final battle with the Joker. Harvey Dent had called to say he was on Fifty-second Boulevard, in a burned-out warehouse. He wanted Gordon to meet him there. Gordon was relieved that Dent was alive, and since Batman was taking care of the Joker, he hurried away.

At the warehouse, Gordon felt danger. He removed his gun from its holster and slowly made his way into the shell of the building.

"Dent?" Gordon called out. He moved to the

staircase and climbed to the second floor.

There he found Barbara, huddled together with their son and daughter. He moved toward them.

Wham!

Dent cracked Gordon over the head with his gun. Gordon slumped to the floor, while Dent took his weapon and grabbed his son.

"This is where they brought her, Gordon," Dent told the commissioner.

"I know. I was here, trying to save her." It had been a devastating night.

Dent turned to Gordon, with only his hideous, dark side showing. "But you didn't save her, did you?"

"You're right; it's my fault Rachel died. Punish me instead."

When Dent made no sign of setting the boy free, a deep voice called out from the shadows.

"Wait." Batman stepped in, closing the gap between Dent and himself. "Gordon's not the only one to blame. What about me? I'm the one who chose the other address."

Dent considered Batman's words.

"Fair enough," he said. "You first." He quickly

flipped his coin, checked the result, and then shot Batman in the stomach. Batman collapsed onto the floor.

Then Dent turned to Commissioner Gordon. "Your turn, Gordon." He tossed his coin up to determine the commissioner's fate.

While Dent's eyes followed the coin, Batman peeled himself off the floor and hurled himself toward Dent. They vanished down into a hole in the floor. There was a terrible crash, followed by a deafening silence. The only sound in the warehouse was that of Dent's coin spinning on the wooden floor.

Dent was lying at the bottom of the pit, his neck broken.

Batman suddenly appeared, swinging from his grapnel hook.

"Thank you," Gordon said.

"You don't have to thank me," Batman replied.

"Yes, I do," Gordon replied.

In the basement of the warehouse, Batman and Gordon stood over Dent's broken body. "The Joker won," Gordon remarked. "He took the best of us and tore him down. People will lose hope." Gordon took a closer look at Dent's scarred face.

Batman reached down and turned Dent's face to show the pristine, good side. "They won't." He looked up at Gordon.

Batman sighed and stood tall next to Gordon. "No. The Joker cannot win. Gotham needs its true hero."

Gordon understood. Batman was going to take the blame for what Dent had done to avenge Rachel. "You? You can't—"

"Yes. I can. You either die a hero or live long enough to see yourself become the villain." Batman handed Gordon his police radio. He wanted Gordon to call his troops.

"They'll hunt you."

Batman smiled. "*You'll* hunt me."

As Batman ran off into the night, the sound of sirens followed him.

"Why are they chasing him?" young James Gordon asked his father.

"Because . . ." Commissioner Gordon wanted

to get the words just right. "He's the hero Gotham deserves, but not the one it needs right now. So we'll hunt him, because he can take it. Because he's not our hero. He's a silent guardian, a watchful protector . . . a dark knight."